"Sugar or cream?"

"Just sugar."

She lifted on tiptoe to the top shelf for the bag of sugar, exposing, he could not help but notice, one smooth curvy hip and a dainty indentation of waistline. Before he knew it, he was beside her, one hand on her skin, the other effortlessly snagging the sugar that had been just out of her reach.

"I don't have a sugar bowl." Of all the things she could have said, this was about the stupidest. But she couldn't help it. His hand on her naked midriff made her an instant idiot.

"I bought all kinds of dishes and treasures for the cottages at the antique store in town," she babbled.

"But not a single sugar bowl," he added.

"Or a creamer."

They stood there at her kitchen counter talking about coffee condiments, and she swore it was turning into the sexiest conversation she'd ever had.

He was so close she could smell the beach on his skin. They moved at the same time, sat across from each other at the little table, sipping coffee. Even though she was famished, the cookies sat on a pretty plate between them untouched.

She wasn't hungry for cookies.

Blue Heaven

by

Cynthia Harrison

Blue Lake, Book 1

Blue Heaven

Cover Art by *Angela Anderson*

The Wild Rose Press, Inc.
PO Box 708
Adams Basin, NY 14410-0708
Visit us at www.thewildrosepress.com

Publishing History
First Champagne Rose Edition, 2013
Print ISBN 978-1-61217-989-6
Digital ISBN 978-1-61217-990-2

Blue Lake, Book 1
Published in the United States of America

Dedication

For my parents, Margorie & William Hines,
both avid readers,
who first taught me the power of the printed word.

I'd like to thank my editor, Dj Hendrickson,
for all her work on my behalf.
Also, much love and thanks to my husband, Al,
for being my rock.
I wouldn't be able to do this without your support,
my love.

Chapter One

"No."

Eva Delacroix sucked in her amazed fury at the loan officer. "Excuse me? Did you just say…"

"I said no. Blue Lake Community Bank can't help you."

For the last ten minutes, the guy in Clark Kent glasses had listened to her explain her business plan for Blue Heaven. His body, she swore, leaned forward with pleasure when she displayed the property title. Where was the red cape when you needed it? She bit her tongue to keep from speaking her thoughts aloud and breathed steadily. Now was not the time for emotion. Now was the time for persuasion.

"I know it's not a very good drawing, but town planning told me anything would do, just to get started." She tried to see the rough sketch through his eyes, tried to imagine what his problem with her delicious and perfect plan could possibly be.

"It's not the drawing."

"What is the problem? I'm sure I can fix it." This plan to remake her family property into a vacation resort had to work. Her last and only option, unless she wanted to move into a senior citizen complex with her mother in Florida.

"You can't stick a second floor on a Bryman bungalow."

An almost undetectable shudder went through his body.

What was his problem? Who was Bryman? And why would he object to a second floor on *her* house? Eva needed this guy to make like Superman and rescue her ramshackle property, but instead he just confused her.

She looked at the nameplate on the banker's desk. Just Daniel. No last names up here in Blue Lake. Everybody was probably related to everybody else. Except her. That hadn't mattered when she'd been a girl. Her extended family surrounded her every summer. Now they were gone and she was alone. And Daniel's face was like a brick wall, determined to keep her out.

"Could I speak to your manager, Daniel?"

"I own this bank." Not a chink in the wall. Not a sign of the sweet guy who'd seemed so charming just ten minutes ago. Something was off. Guys in their thirties did not own banks, and, when confronted with the full force of her determined enthusiasm, their faces did not usually resemble stone.

"So you own the whole place?" She looked around the room, seeking a way to get him on her side. There had to be something she could say or do to show him she was right and he was wrong. The brick wall he'd erected meant flirting would not work. She had to make him feel the way she did about Blue Heaven. She had to get him into her corner. Okay, his father probably owned this bank, allowing little rich boy Daniel to run it and pretend he was important. He'd been leading her on so that he could say no. A power trip thing. That had to be it. She needed the words right now that would allow them both a win.

"I have a partner."

"Your dad?" Those were not the right words. They were exactly the wrong words. Damn.

An expression passed over his face, like he was holding back a sneeze. Then he recovered and his face went blank again.

"No," he said.

She could tell he was never going to say yes. Something with the father. She blew it big-time. So she shot for the moon.

"Would your partner listen to my proposal?"

"He's semi-retired. I make those decisions."

The blood in her veins pounded against her temples. She began rethinking the whole "keep it in the community" idea she'd had about remodeling Blue Heaven, but she kept her face neutral, mirroring his. She'd give it one more try.

"The cottages and the bungalow have been sitting empty for years. It will be good for the town if I opened them up again. Good for tourism."

"Not feasible." Daniel shook his head.

His dorky glasses weren't that cute, Eva thought. *If he owns a bank, why doesn't he get corrective surgery?*

"Will you explain to me why not?" In her mind, the plan was perfection, but she was thinking a few steps ahead. Maybe things would go better at the next bank if he detailed his problem with her proposal. She could amend her proposal if his objections made sense. Highly doubtful, but she was always open to suggestions.

He sighed and pushed his glasses up his nose. He drew her financial sheets out of the fan of paperwork.

"Are you employed, Ms. Delacroix?"

Since he had her financial information in his hand, he knew the answer. "It's Eva." She decided to remind him that she was living in Blue Lake now, a member of the community and a person with a first name, if not an actual job. "I'm not currently employed. I plan to be self-employed. I'm going to work on my property, first fixing it up, then renting out the cottages. To tourists." All of this was self-explanatory, or so she thought. Maybe he was dumber than he looked. Pity, really. She couldn't help herself, she liked his looks. But thank stars not his personality.

He carefully paged through her financial paperwork. It didn't take long.

"I'm sorry, Eva, but in this economy, we aren't offering mortgages to unemployed folks."

Okay. Now she was getting somewhere. Although this was not what she wanted to hear, she should know what she was up against. Right now, things were tough in Michigan, but there were programs in place to help stimulate the state economy. She had to fit into one of them. "What about that thing the President is doing, helping people who can't pay their mortgages?"

"To re-mortgage at a lower rate, you need to have a mortgage in the first place. Which you don't."

"Can't I acquire one?"

"We can't count unemployment payments as income. So you have no source of income to pay us back. Is there a way you can get a job?"

Like she hadn't been trying. She'd been to every advertising agency in Detroit, and a few in Chicago and New York, too. After almost a year, she'd come to the conclusion that the advertising game was changing and that she should, too.

Turning Blue Heaven into a tourist spot *was* her idea of a job, and it was a good one. "I've got two months to fix up those cottages so I can rent them out this summer."

"It's not a bad plan, except for the part about adding a second floor on your bungalow. But we're cutting to the bone these days. And you're high-risk."

"I'm not!" Eva wasn't sure why she took his words so personally. This was business. And right now, real estate was risky. But two acres on a Great Lake waterfront was not just any old piece of real estate.

"I'm sorry." Daniel pulled his phone from his pocket and glanced at it in one efficient motion. "I've got a lunch appointment."

That was it. Well, maybe this was the only bank in Blue Lake, but it wasn't the only bank in northern Michigan.

Daniel held the gleaming glass door open for her, and they walked into the parking lot together. The spring day had turned warm. The branches of the cherry trees lining Main Street were full of tightly furled buds. The air felt full of promise and possibility. Even though Daniel doubted her, she knew she was finally on the right track with her life. She'd find the money to make her dream come true somewhere.

"I'm sorry, Eva." Daniel stopped at a sleek black Lexus parked next to her red Mustang. "I wish I could help. I mean that."

Okay, so maybe he was a nice guy. Just doing his job. He seemed like he wanted to say more, but she couldn't tell what because his glasses had darkened in the sun, making his eyes unreadable. He reached to shake her hand and when she touched his skin she felt like a tree bursting into bloom. *What was that about?* Sitting across the desk from him, she'd noticed he was very good-looking. But now, standing here in the fecund street, she felt a strong wave of energy flow between them.

Probably just a reaction to her utter lack of a sex life.

"My advice," he said, breaking the handshake without having seemed to feel the same urgent current she had, "is to find a job. Any job. There's a Walmart in Port Huron."

This suggestion cooled her sex jets right off. Cold rain fell on her heart's parade. He didn't understand. He could not see the potential. Ah well, his loss.

****

Eva was tempted to shoot right down the highway out of Blue Lake and into the next town with a bank. Then her stomach grumbled; she hadn't eaten breakfast. If there had been a drive-thru fast food place in Blue Lake, she'd have used it. But the little town had kept its old-fashioned character, with not a chain store or restaurant to be seen on Main Street. During the winter months there was only one place open for lunch. She pulled into Fast Eddie's Bar and Grill and noticed with chagrin the black Lexus parked close to the back entrance.

She walked in, and as her eyes adjusted to the dark bar, Eva saw Daniel sitting in a corner with a blonde woman wearing a green suit. His girlfriend? Didn't matter. Determined to stay positive, she sat at the bar, as far away from Downer Daniel as possible.

After she gave her order to an older man she

figured must be Eddie, Eva noticed three ancient retirees staring at her from the other end of the bar. She felt a little bit out of place, like a specimen under glass, but took off her jacket anyway.

"You're that gal living in the Delacroix place, hey?" one of them said.

From the corner of her eye, she saw Daniel notice her. She took a sip of her soda and nodded to the speaker.

"I'm Eva Delacroix," she said.

"Knew your granddaddy," another of the trio mentioned. "It'd kill him to see how the place has gone to ruin."

Eva listened to the sizzle of her burger on the grill. She was so hungry it would be gone in four bites. She ripped open the bag of chips Eddie had set down with her soda.

"I'm fixing them up," she said after inhaling a few chips and taking a sip of her soda. "And they're not that bad."

Three hoots of varying range rippled over the sound of her crunching. "Hope you brought buckets of dough," one of them said as Eddie delivered her hamburger. She bit into it without replying.

Halfway through her burger, Daniel approached.

"Hi, Eva." There went that electricity crackling between them again. At least she felt it. Maybe he didn't. Maybe it wasn't "between" them at all, but a half-figment of her imagination.

"Hi." After the brief greeting, she took another bite of her burger, realizing her hunger was for more than just food. Even though he put a damper on her day, he had also used some type of superhero magnetism on her hand. And now the air between them had a tension she could almost see. She had to stop this. Just because she was lonely and he was cute, she didn't have to let it ruin her lunch.

"You following me?" His smile meant he put some work into being witty. She gave him points for trying. Maybe he felt the same thick need in the air between them that she did. Maybe he'd felt something zing through their touching hands back there in the bank parking lot after all. Maybe he felt what she felt, a totally inappropriate reaction to a person she had only met this morning, hardly knew, and didn't really like.

"Don't flatter yourself," she teased back. "Just grabbing lunch before I head over to Bank of America in Port Huron." She took another big bite of her juicy burger.

He sat on the stool next to her, shaking his head at Eddie, signaling he wasn't staying long. Too bad. She'd had a half-formed hope he'd change his mind about that loan. What did he want? A date? How would that be? Could she forgive him for turning down her loan application? She shook her head to get the foolishness out, set her burger down on its plate and wiped her mouth with a napkin. It felt rough against her lips. How would it be to kiss Daniel's lips? *Shut up!* She told herself, looking at everything in the bar except him.

"I'd like to see Blue Heaven restored as much as everybody else in town," he said, bringing her eyes back to his. "But you can't mess with the integrity of a Bryman design."

From behind the bar, Eddie snorted.

Daniel ignored him.

This was the second time he'd mentioned Bryman.

He must be the guy who built Blue Heaven back in the 1920s. Why she should care about some dead guy's "integrity of design" was unclear.

Eva pushed her plate away, her appetite gone. She was beginning to think he turned down her loan application to stop her from building the addition, not because she was high risk. Eva unzipped her purse and grabbed her wallet.

"Did I hear them right?"

Eva looked up to see the woman Daniel had been sitting with now standing next to him. She held Eva's eye and gestured to the three codgers with her thumb.

"You're Eva Delacroix?"

"Yep," Eva said. She pulled a twenty out of her wallet, put it on the bar, and turned her attention to Daniel's friend.

"Well, hi," the woman in green smiled, her tone warm. "I'm Jane Augustine, from Blue Lake Realty. I brokered—"

"I know." Eva recognized the name. This was the woman who had helped her father buy out his sisters when they'd insisted on selling their shares in Blue Heaven.

"Well, ladies, I need to get back to work," Daniel said. He stood up and waved to the guys down the bar.

"I owe you one, Jane," he said as he left. Jane took the seat Daniel vacated and ordered a glass of Chardonnay. "Bring Eva a glass, too, Eddie, and put it on my tab."

"No, thanks." Eva was grateful that somebody in town was finally willing to offer her something, but she really needed to find a loan.

"I would ask if you want to unload the old place,"

Jane said, sipping her wine, "but I hear you've got other ideas."

"Yeah, I do. Thanks anyway."

"Got your work cut out for you."

Eva nodded. She'd been at it for a week already, cleaning windows, tearing out old carpet, washing walls.

"You wouldn't happen to know a roofer, would you?" The cottages had missing shingles. Every roof needed to be replaced, including her bungalow's, after she added that second floor.

Jane pulled out her cell phone and scrolled, then took a card out of her purse and wrote on the back.

"Thanks." In true Blue Lake fashion, Jane had only written a first name, *Frank*, and then a phone number. As she slid from her bar stool, Eva grabbed her jacket. She'd like to stay and talk to Jane, who seemed like a nice person, but she had business to take care of first.

"I might be able to get you that loan."

Eva stilled, one arm in her jacket, the other dangling. "How?"

"You'd never know this by the way Daniel behaves, but my daddy still owns fifty-one percent of that bank. And I know he'd think it best to keep your business in Blue Lake."

Eva slid her arm from the jacket sleeve and sat back down.

"Everybody in the county has been waiting for the day Blue Heaven could be restored," Jane said. "Your daddy used to come in here with me for lunch and he'd be full of plans for the place." Here Jane paused and reached a hand over the bar to cover Eva's. "I was sorry to hear he passed."

Eva nodded and Jane sipped her wine. Eva had heard those plans many times. It was a big part of the reason she was here, attempting to do this thing. Her dad had planted the seed, and his dream lived on in Eva. She really believed, as Jane did, that opening Blue Heaven to paying guests would be a boon to the entire town.

"So why doesn't Daniel get it?"

"Really? You don't know?" Jane looked amused. "Eddie, bring this woman a glass of wine."

Eddie poured the wine and put it down in front of Eva.

"I'm sorry," Eva said. "I don't want to be rude, but I really need to get financing for my project before I celebrate." She let the wine sit there on the bar.

Jane smiled and pulled out her phone. "Daddy?" she said after pressing the keypad. "I need a favor."

A short conversation ensued, with Jane's back to Eva so she couldn't hear much of what was said. Then Jane shut her phone, promising Eva the paperwork would be typed up and ready to sign in ten minutes.

Eva felt a little like Cinderella meeting her fairy godmother, but she decided not to question the fortunate turn her day had taken. It was about time for something to go right in life. She sipped her glass of wine, just to be polite. It was surprisingly delicious. She took another small sip, which had nothing to do with the fact that she was a tad nervous about how Daniel would react when she waltzed back into the bank and claimed her cash. This reminded her that she still didn't know why he cared about that guy named Bryman—and her bungalow—so much.

Eva clinked glasses with Jane. "Thank you," she

said. After a final token sip, Eva set her wine glass back on the dark polished wood of the bar.

"Why is Daniel so territorial about my property?"

"He's a Bryman," Jane said, rolling her eyes.

Bryman. Eva had a sense before that Daniel talked as if this unknown Bryman was another Frank Lloyd Wright or something, but now everything clicked into place.

"He's related to the architect who designed Blue Heaven," Eva said.

"His great-granddaddy," Jane confirmed.

Interesting. Eva took another sip of her wine, without thinking, and then set it as far out of reach as possible.

"I know you want to keep a clear head," Jane said, eyeing the distant unfinished glass of wine. "But we have to give our clerk time to type up the paperwork."

"After the deal's signed, I'd be happy to buy you an entire bottle of wine," Eva said.

A smile softened Jane's face. In her designer suit and high heels, Jane appeared a super-competent businesswoman, but her smile transformed her into someone else. Maybe a new friend.

"I'll take you up on that," Jane said.

"I still don't understand why Daniel would spite the entire town just because he's afraid I'll botch the renovation."

"He'd call it a restoration. Bit of a control freak. But it's not his fault." Jane eyed Eva's glass of wine. "Hit me one more time, Eddie," she said, pushing her empty glass toward the bartender.

"Why isn't it his fault?" Eva asked, since she had to wait for Jane to drink yet another glass of wine.

"That he's so controlling, I mean."

"Daniel wanted to be an architect, too. He was in college in Ann Arbor when he was called home. Family tragedy." She set down her wine glass and crossed her arms. "I think buying up and renovating every Bryman home in town became kind of an obsession with him."

Eva wondered what the tragedy was, but she didn't want to pry. She thought about Daniel's face in the bank that morning when she'd mentioned his father. It hit her all at once, like most of her verbal gaffs. Something bad had happened to Daniel's father.

Chapter Two

Daniel took the loan papers for Eva's financing from his secretary, and looked them over. Everything was legal, if not ethical. Jane had her father wrapped around her little finger, so old man Augustine fast-tracking Eva's paperwork didn't pique his curiosity as much as Jane taking an interest in Eva. He felt an old stir of discomfort.

Just then, Eva sashayed in the front door of the bank like a satisfied cat who'd just licked clean a bowl of cream. She walked toward him, hips swinging, a smile on her face. This woman demanded notice. And he did. Notice her. He was human, after all. He handed her the documents and indicated a chair. He sat across from her, watching her read. She took her time on the fine print. Smart and pretty all in one petite package.

"One missed payment and we begin foreclosure."

"I can read." She signed the pages and pushed them toward him. "Anything else?"

"Good luck." This time he turned away from her swaying hips and her pert ass. He had to find a way to stop her from ruining Blue Heaven.

Once Eva left the building, and he saw her pull out of the lot, he got into his car and drove to the state park. Not because it was next to Eva's property, but because running on the beach relaxed him.

He changed his loafers for the running shoes he

kept in the trunk and headed down to the pier. The spring air made goose bumps pop up on his bare arms as he neared the water. He made his way down the beach from the pier steps. Despite the proof on his skin, he didn't feel the outer weather. His lungs filled with air full of positive freshwater ions. He sought to calm the turmoil inside, created when a certain hurricane named Eva had blown into town.

Before he knew it, he'd jogged almost to the trickle of river that ran through the middle of town. As he turned and headed back to the pier, he could hear the faint sound of construction.

He sprinted the final length of sand, taking Eva's rickety steps up from the beach instead of going on to the park. Frank Smith pried and pulled at the shingles on her bungalow's roof, tossing them to the ground.

"Hey!" Daniel yelled at Frank. "Hang on a minute," he said, when the roofer looked down. Frank had done a fair amount of work for Daniel, so he tended to listen when given a direct order.

"What are you doing here?" Eva emerged from the bungalow as Frank climbed down the ladder. Her hair, whipped by the wind, stuck in her lip gloss. For a minute, Daniel lost his train of thought. He had to restrain himself from tucking the errant curl behind her ear. She was so pretty, even when anger puckered her forehead.

"I was just making sure Frank is using cedar shingles." He said the first thing that popped into his head.

Frank walked toward his truck.

"Hey? Frank?" Eva said to his retreating back. The roofer didn't turn around but he held up a cell phone, indicating he was making a call.

"He's calling the builder about my second floor," Eva said, confirming Daniel's worst fears.

"Shouldn't you get those cottages in shape for paying customers first?"

Frank ambled back up to them. He nodded to Eva, handing Daniel a cedar shingle.

Daniel sensed Eva bristle at the way her roofer took orders from him, so he didn't ask Frank for the name of the general contractor he planned to bring on board. There were no general contractors in the area, except him. Frank would have had to go to someone in Port Huron. Daniel fought the urge to openly fume at this missed opportunity. Inside, he seethed. *He* should be in charge of renovating Blue Heaven. *His notion* that no second floor was needed should be the prevailing opinion.

"These are the shingles for the cottages," she said. "Right, Frank?"

"Riggghhht," Frank said, shaking his head and moving the ladder from the bungalow over to the closest cottage. He climbed atop and started tearing down shingles.

"You'll need a cottage to live in if you plan to remove your roof," Daniel said. He was sure Frank had been preparing to tear off a huge chunk of her bungalow's roof, and was silently thankful he'd averted disaster—for now.

"Yeah," she said, trying to be cheerful when he could tell by her tone that she was anything but happy about having to delay her crazy plan for that second story. Somehow he had to find a way to talk some sense into her.

****

Eva turned from Daniel. He was wrong about the addition, wrong to deny her a loan, but right when it came to prioritizing the work. And he had a tragic past, which tipped the balance in his favor.

She let her fists fall from her hips, raised one hand to shade her eyes as she took a good long look at the water winking in the late afternoon sun. As usual, just breathing in the big water, so endless it looked like an ocean, relaxed her. It wasn't easy admitting, even to herself, that he was right, and that she'd been about to make a huge mistake.

"Did Jane tell you I restore these places? The Bryman homes?" Daniel asked.

His voice, so full of eager hope and so clearly showing his vulnerability, made her ache for him even without knowing the whole story of his past. It was kind of him to pretend she hadn't been about to make a huge mistake by tearing the roof off her bungalow before she had a livable cottage to stay in.

"Why are you so set on adding a second story to this house?"

"It was my dad's dream." She turned away, looked again at the water. "Jane told me your great-grandfather designed and built this place. I think my great-grandpa helped him. Those are the family stories, anyhow, that he worked alongside the builder."

"I didn't know that." Daniel was quiet for a minute, the expression on his face going from thoughtful to cheery. "So if they worked together, we can too."

Eva had no idea what he was talking about, but before she could frame a question, he said, "I'd be happy to offer you the benefit of my experience renovating Bryman properties."

"Listen, Daniel, thanks for the offer. Really. It's very generous of you. Except the problem remains. You don't want me to build my second story."

"Why would you even want to? It was your dad's dream. Is it your dream, too?"

Not exactly, but it was a good Plan B. "Guests can gather for a glass of wine or to play a board game in front of a cozy fire on rainy days or cool evenings."

"Really? On vacation? People do that?"

Her eyes turned from the water. He had taken off his glasses and was polishing them on his T-shirt.

"In my family, aunts, uncles, cousins, we'd each choose a cottage, but everyone would congregate in the bungalow for meals and games, movies and reading."

"No brothers or sisters?" He put his glasses back on.

"Only child." She almost said "What about you?" but then let it go. They both turned toward the stairs leading up the bluff. After a few steps along the beach, Daniel stopped.

"I admit I don't like the idea of adding to an existing structure," Daniel said. "But I'm also being practical. You need to make your first loan payment in two months. I didn't like the terms of that contract. You could easily lose everything if you aren't careful. I believe you'll find that the money may not stretch as far as you think."

She was walking a bit ahead of him, so turned back to face him. "I appreciate your honesty. I have to admit you make some good points." She dropped her gaze to the sand, dug the toe of her sneaker into it. "I know you've done lots of renovations in town, but have you ever tried to build an addition? Have you ever given modernizing and expanding an original design a shot?"

"I built a second story once," he said. "An airplane bungalow on Sugar Street. Completely gutted by fire. We knocked the burned out shell down and rebuilt it stick by stick."

She looked up at him. His face came alive when he talked about building. So different from that brick wall of an expression he wore at the bank. "But that house was designed as a two story. There's a certain integrity to keeping to the original design."

"That's what they call it? An airplane?"

"Yeah. Or sometimes story and a half."

"Well, there you go. I only need a half on top. One big room."

She wanted to win him over. For some reason she didn't understand, it seemed important that their visions align.

He shook his head, not even glancing at the bungalow. "It's your house. You do what you want with it. But be careful. Everything, electrical, plumbing, heat, it all costs twice what you think."

"How did you know I need all that work done?"

He shrugged. "I've been doing this a long time."

She wondered if he had a girlfriend. Apparently he and Jane were just business associates.

"I know an electrician." He took her arm when she tried to walk ahead again. His touch was gentle, her skin warmed under this soft request to stop and talk a minute more.

"It's a small town." His hand dropped from her arm when he realized she would stay. She missed it a little bit. "Everybody knows everybody else. Including all their business."

Hmmm. She could ask Jane all about Daniel's business when they went out for that bottle of wine.

"These guys are competent. Dependable. There's an excellent painter who restores wood and repairs plaster. We have a plumber in town who could use a paycheck. I even know a guy who will retrofit all your steam heaters so they work like modern but..."

"Let me guess, maintain the original integrity."

She couldn't help it, when he grinned and nodded, she smiled back at him. She understood him now. He really cared about these places his relative had designed and built way back when. There was something sweet about that. She might be in trouble, because something about him turned the key in her ignition. And revved it up.

"I appreciate all your advice." She wondered if he was thinking similar sexy thoughts about her. "But I have a budget and a timeframe, and unless your people are willing to work with my plan, I'll find my own crew." She spoke with authority, trying to keep a clear head around this guy who made her feel warm and fuzzy inside.

"I'm sure whatever you're planning, our local guys will try their hardest to accommodate you. Everyone could use the work, to be honest. And, like I said, I'm always happy to offer advice."

"Thanks." She blinked in an effort to focus on his words and not his toned arms. She could see the muscles bulge and tighten right through his white T-shirt.

****

"There's an obese cat in your shed," Bob, the paint and plaster guy, said. A full crew had shown up that morning and the cottages, if being turned inside out was any indication, were well on their way to restoration. Every cottage door was open, every little yard space had a set of tools lined up outside the door. Rotted wood and crumbling toilet seats, rusted pipes, a broken cupboard, all were being hauled and dumped into a giant green garbage bin by competent-looking men.

Eva was just glad someone other than she had gone into the cobweb-ridden shed. Bob looked very young, but seemed in control. He'd already set up the shed as construction headquarters, and she noticed that a lot of the guys conferred with him before ripping anything out of the cottages.

"Whose cat?" Eva asked.

"Yours," Bob said.

"Oh." Eva mentally added cat food to her shopping list.

"Keeps the rodent population down," Bob said.

After negotiating with these guys, she'd agreed to offer them what folks kept referring to as "day's wages" which she finally figured out was one hundred dollars cash for every day they worked. A bargain, but after she'd struck it, she'd realized it didn't include taxes. She'd figure how to pay taxes later. Meanwhile, time estimates were spot on. If all went well, the cottages should be ready for occupancy ahead of schedule. And then she could build her second story.

As she handed Bob the paint chips she'd picked out for the cottages, a different pastel shade for each, she casually asked him how he knew Daniel.

"He's my brother," Bob said, stuffing the paint

21

samples into his back pocket and heading off to Port Huron for supplies.

Eva took advantage of the gorgeous sunshine to walk on the beach. Nobody was out yet, the weather was too raw. Windy with a chill in the air. Well, maybe one other person was brave enough, she thought, her heart now beating faster as she recognized the figure running toward her. Daniel.

Chapter Three

His hair was short, so it didn't ruffle at all in the wind, unlike her own, which flew all around her face. She caught the strands up in one hand and walked toward Daniel.

Lake Huron churned and slapped against the rocky shore, imitating the way her heart churned in her chest. Daniel stopped in front of her, his mouth an easy grin, his words saying hello like they were old pals.

She returned his greeting, noticed his muscled legs, his strong arms, his deep, rich breath. She really needed to get a grip. Her attraction had come on strong enough now that she figured he'd either ask her out, or he wouldn't. And if he did, they'd fight over her addition, so it was better if he didn't. Probably.

"How's Bob working out?"

"Fine, but you didn't mention he was your brother."

"Oh. Well, is that a problem?"

Since the work day was more than half over, she guessed it wasn't. "Maybe," she said, thinking of the cash payments.

"Really? Why?"

She explained the tax issue.

"I'm thinking of asking Bob to take a check and disburse the funds to the crew himself, that way I have something for the IRS."

"Should not be a problem." As Daniel lifted his hand to sweep his hair from his forehead, his shoulders strained against the material of his white T-shirt. She couldn't help but surmise that he must do some other form of exercise besides running, because, for a banker, he was quite fit. She bet his arms around her would be strong. They'd make her feel safe.

"You have an accountant, right?"

She brought her wandering mind back to the conversation.

She didn't have an accountant, but she'd hire one today. Somebody had to figure out how much she'd have to add to Bob's paycheck in order to cover taxes.

"I already told Bob he could work for cash," she admitted.

"I'll straighten it out for you."

"No, that's okay. I'll speak to Bob." Eva felt her heart speed up and her stomach clench. Was it from attraction or irritation or both? This was her project, not his. She took long calming breaths of lake air as they walked. They stopped together at the rickety steps leading up to her property.

"You have good insurance, right?" he said, eyeing the steps.

"I do." She'd taken care of that earlier today when she realized she had a crew of men on her property who'd need to be covered in case of injury.

He went over to the steps and pulled lightly at a board. She'd already noted that several had bad spots, splits, a bit of rot, but this one fell completely apart in his hands. She didn't remember them being in such disrepair when she and her mom had come here last summer to scatter her dad's ashes.

"I can fix these for you."

She must quit staring at his muscled arms. She focused on his hair, glinting in the sun. You didn't see that color of natural blonde on men much downstate. *Stop it right now.*

"I'm sure someone on the crew can handle it," she said."Who'd you bring on?" he asked casually, still inspecting the steps. They were all the names he'd given her, so she didn't understand why he was shaking his head.

"You don't have a carpenter. Nobody who really knows wood, except Bob, and he's going to be busy restoring the wood in the cottages."

She thought about how her insurance premiums would skyrocket if someone crashed through a rotted beach step. And the way Daniel kept prodding them, they were all likely to collapse in a heap before he was finished.

"Honest to God, it would be a pleasure to help." Daniel continued poking and prodding the rotted wood.

"You didn't give me the name of a carpenter. "He didn't look at her. She wondered if he had omitted that information on purpose. So he could be the carpenter. So he could oversee the renovation."What about the bank? Don't you have a real job?"

"I'm easing out of my role at the bank."

"You're leaving?"

He nodded and finally turned around, dusting his hands on his jeans. A huge grin split his face as he looked into her eyes. "I've been training my replacement for when Bob goes to college in the fall."

He was still smiling. He had really nice teeth. Was there anything about him that was not perfect? Well, he wore glasses, but then, they suited him.

"Why?" She bit her bottom lip. Had she been too intrusive?

"My family came up to Michigan from Georgia about a hundred years ago." He went back to pulling and prodding at the rotting steps. More silver wood fell to the sand. "After he became an architect, Bryman went south every winter, to oversee the homes he designed down there. That's my next move."

"You're moving to Georgia?" She had to stop repeating his words, but they made no sense. She collected the discarded the pile of wood, moving it closer to the bluff leading to the house, away from the sandy beach and the running path.

"For the winter months. I've already bought a couple of Bryman properties there. In pretty bad shape, too." It was like she could read his mind by the tone of his voice. He loved a challenge. They had that in common. She tried to pull off a board of her own.

He came over and helped her pull the stubborn step off the foundation board. When their shoulders touched, she could have sworn he leaned into her on purpose. *Keep leaning.*

"I could use a hammer. And some gloves," he said, but they stayed where they were, pulling at the loose boards together, letting arms, hands, shoulders touch.

"Ow." A splinter of wood spiked the pad of her thumb. She pulled it out quickly, blotting the bead of blood on her jeans.

"So is it just you and Bob? You're like his guardian?"

He nodded, but kept working, kept his eyes on the job, and didn't explain.

She began to form a mental picture of Daniel as a dad. He was young, but solid. Kind but not a pushover. Good job. Stable life. Perfect dad material. She forced herself to stop the direction her thoughts were heading. Since Marcus shot her down, she'd been licking her wounds, barely even dating. Now all that baby lust came flooding back. Because of Daniel.

"I'll go up and get some tools and do this right," Daniel said. He stopped working and, looking down at the sand, said, "After our parents died, we sort of grew up together. My grandparents were still alive then, so they helped."

Eva's heart softened, but she kept her face as neutral as possible. Guys hated pity. So did she. She never knew what to say to the people at her dad's funeral. Some of them cried so hard she had to console them, when it was her mom and her who were the bereaved.

"What happened?" The words escaped before she could take them back.

"Car accident," Daniel said. He kicked at the neat pile of wood they'd been building, avoiding her eyes. "My dad died instantly, but our mother hung on, in a coma, for weeks." He tried to keep his voice neutral; she tried not to hug him. He looked like he needed one. Or maybe that was just wishful thinking on her part. No wonder he always tried to fix everything. No wonder he tried to keep whatever pieces of his family were left intact and exactly the same.

He held his large hands to frame the partially dismantled steps like a camera lens. "I'd make them wider," he said. She noticed his hands were banged up for a banker, his fingers a little thick. Better hands for a

27

hammer than a keyboard. His thumb nail on the right hand was smashed, a little deformed. So, another flaw. But, like the glasses, an endearing one. "And build a handrail on both sides. That might even lower your insurance premiums."

"Sounds expensive," she said, but in a soft tone. It had been so much easier to treat him in a business-like manner when he was dressed in a suit and tie. When she had not known his history.

"This—" He still kept his hands in a frame of the stairway in his head. "—leads to a Bryman property. I'd do it for free."

This guy was either way generous or…what? What did he stand to gain? She covered her doubts by teasing him. "Don't you mind changing the integrity of the beach steps?"

"Oh, these old things have been rebuilt plenty of times," he said. "Weather. Water. People. Tears 'em up every decade or so."

He climbed up what was left of the steps, stopping and turning to hold out a hand to help her up the ones they'd pulled loose.

She took his hand just in case, but focused on balancing on her own. When he would have continued walking toward the bungalow, she pulled him back. Which is when she realized they were still holding hands. And it felt nice. Warm and tingly, not a sexy shock like the first time they'd touched. She reluctantly released her grip on his hand.

"Look at this with me for a minute," she said.

They stood side by side, staring at the house. Flaking paint made it look like a wrinkled old lady. The cement stoop begged to be turned into a big front porch.

The squat roof wanted to be a room full of people. She could feel it.

"Can't you just picture a second floor? The overhang could be the roof of a big porch? And upstairs there'd be windows to show off the lake view, with comfy furniture, and a fireplace and books and tables for eating and playing board games on rainy days?"

He seemed to consider what she said and finally, reluctantly, agreed. "Yes, I can see how this might be turned into an airplane-style bungalow." He was quiet for a beat, while she basked in the sweetness of winning him over. "But that's not what Bryman built."

Okay, so she hadn't won. Still, he'd seen what she'd seen. Their inner visions had agreed.

"Maybe he meant to," she said. "Maybe he ran out of money. It was the Depression, after all."

"We'll never know. Unless you've got the blueprints stashed somewhere." Daniel stood with his arms folded across his slim waist, still looking at her house.

She laughed. "Nope." Then she sighed. "It's just...that's the part about coming up here that was so special. My aunts and cousins and us, we'd all have our own cottages, but every meal, we'd gather in the bungalow. And at night, we'd all be there together."

"I heard your aunts insisted your dad buy them out."

"They wanted him to sell his share too. That way they'd get the money faster." All the anger and sorrow her dad's decision to keep Blue Heaven had caused—one day she had a big, happy extended family, and the next nobody but Mom and Dad. Then just Mom—made her yearn to create a family of her own.

Chapter Four

Daniel had never been inside the bungalow. He wished she'd ask him in. If he fixed her beach stairs and her accounting problem with Bob, maybe she would. There was something in her that pulled him toward her. And it wasn't just Blue Heaven.

While Eva went to the truck of her car to unload a box of what she called "treasures" he spoke briefly to Bob.

"Let me get that," he said, taking the awkward box from Eva. Her arms were so delicate, pale and soft, but she wanted to do everything. He admired the way she'd pitched in with the beach steps, showing she wasn't afraid of hard work.

"Careful," she said when the box he held clinked. Glass, he figured.

She went back to her car and pulled out another, smaller box, affording him a perfect view of her sweet rounded backside. Then she slammed her trunk and he thought, *Just my luck. When I'm finally leaving town, someone comes along who makes me want to stay.*

Eva, carrying her box of fragile cargo, was beautiful in the way some women are, the ones who don't know it. It was a quiet sort of beauty. Well, until she got excited about her project. Then her face came alive. *Hold on*, he cautioned himself. *She might be pretty but she isn't practical.* Then he thought about why that would matter. He had enough common sense for both of them. If only she'd let him use it. If only she'd let him help.

He carefully adjusted his box, and opened the door for her.

"Would you like a tour?" she asked.

He walked in, finally right where he wanted to be.

"Just set these down over here," she said, indicating a worn and scarred registration counter, a huge slab of old wood that spanned the walls end to end. It had an old-fashioned flip hinge, and, made from the same wood, an ancient set of pigeon holes were anchored to the wall on the other side of the counter.

He ran his hand over the wood.

"It's awful. I'll need to replace it." Eva settled her box next to his.

"I think this is an old oak, right from the river." Daniel carefully ran his hand over the thick slab of wood.

"Really?" She didn't seem impressed. So he worked a little harder. He wanted to impress her.

"Yeah, I think Bryman took the tree trunk and sanded it down. Look at the grain of the wood."

"Isn't it weird to be an architect *and* a builder? Not just one or the other?" She came over to where he stood and ran a slow hand along the wood. He tried not to think about her slow hands on his body. He forced himself to think about practical things. Like, at least now she knew to watch for splinters. That was something. She also had courage. To start a project like this in the current economy. There was for sure more to Eva Delacroix than just a pretty face.

"I don't know," he answered her question honestly.

He hated that he'd never gotten a formal education, but he'd learned to just admit when he didn't know something. "Maybe it was the times. Maybe he thought only he could get certain things right. From the few letters we have, I know he loved working with wood as much as he did drawing blueprints."

"And you do, too." He nodded even though she wasn't looking at him, but still staring down at the wooden registration counter as if it would eventually give up its secrets.

"All I see are a bunch of gouges and water marks," she admitted. That was fine. He'd teach her to see beneath the surface. If she'd let him. An idea had been growing since he'd seen her on the beach, but he wasn't exactly sure how to bring it up. She was so territorial, and rightly so, when it came to Blue Heaven. He'd wanted this property for a very long time. It had pained him to see the slow deterioration after the family stopped coming. When he'd heard Eva's dad had died, he'd hoped her mother would put it on the market. She didn't, but he could work with what he had. Right now, that was a little piece of Eva's attention. He intended to make that attention grow. He needed to oversee this project. He had to. Nobody else would do it better. Nobody else would keep her from destroying historically accurate floor plans.

"Here's where the staircase would go," she said, indicating a perfect spot next to the entry door. He hated that he could see it. That her passion made him compromise everything he believed in.

"And through here is the kitchen."

Early 1950s re-do, but the knotty pine cabinets were original. She led him through the room before he could take a closer look.

"And this is the living room…"

Except for a ladder, the living room was empty. She'd pulled up the carpet to reveal original wood flooring. She'd washed the windows, which were mostly original glass. She'd even shined the crystals hanging from what looked like an original light fixture in the center of the room.

Daniel pulled the ladder over and climbed the rung to inspect the fixture.

"Original," he said. "This particular globe hasn't been made since 1943."

"But the chain's a little rusty. I was thinking of getting a new one. Or spray painting it so it matched the rest of the brass."

Daniel came down off the ladder.

"It can be cleaned. Try not to replace anything. Please."

She needed him, she just didn't know it yet.

"This room's empty because I'm going to strip the floor and refinish it."

"Perfect," he said. "And it's in good shape. No termites."

"You can tell that from just touching a window sash?"

He'd come down off the ladder to inspect the windows. The sashes were bad, but not the worst he'd seen.

"I was thinking I'd need to replace those?"

"They can be repaired," he said.

"Next you're going to put yourself on my payroll," she said.

"Oh, that reminds me. I spoke to Bob about your

tax situation. Tell your accountant to cut one check to him every week and he'll take care of the rest."

"I told you I'd speak to Bob."

"Really? I don't remember that."

"Because you were too busy plotting how to take charge of my renovation."

"Restoration. And I don't want to 'take charge,' but I do want to help."

She looked miffed at the correction to her terminology.

"I'm sorry." Those two words usually went a long way with women.

Her sweet face softened. He'd bet a Benjamin she was remembering his family history. He wished she wouldn't. He'd rather be admired for his expertise than pitied for his situation.

"I've got an idea," he said.

"Okay," she said, but he could tell by her tone that what she really meant was "No way."

He took a deep breath, still wondering where to start.

"Want a coffee while we talk?"

Relieved and grateful she didn't kick him to the curb, he vowed to be more sensitive to the fact that this was her Bryman house, her project, not his. And that she didn't seem all that interested in taking the advice or the help he'd offered so far.

He followed her back into the small kitchen and took a seat at the chrome-rimmed table, topped with shiny yellow Formica meant to mimic marble. He wasn't great with décor, but this table looked earlier than 1950s. Maybe 30s or 40s. It sort of blended with the avocado green appliances. More or less.

"So, you're bringing Blue Heaven back to its original intended purpose," he said, looking out the little window the table sat up against, probably for its view of the lake.

"I'm not sure this place was ever really used as a business."

"Yep. When the Depression settled in, your great-grandfather, Louis Delacroix, lost his job and decided to move his whole family up here."

"How the heck do you know that?"

"Family legend. Not a lot of proof, other than county records. But I've found postcards. A few letters. Stuff like that. Anecdotal evidence."

"So, what's the rest? I mean, I know he had six kids, including my grandfather, but how long was he in business? And how did he pick this place?"

"The main house was built, and my great-grandfather, Vance Bryman, added the cottages as an afterthought, with the idea that Louis could rent them out and make his living that way. One story says he turned your side room, which was supposed to be a big family gathering room, into an office."

"Wow," she said.

"And then you said that your family stories tell that Louis worked with Vance? That they actually did some of the construction together?"

"That's just a legend. I have no evidence at all, not even anecdotal."

He'd hooked her. Everyone loves family stories. And, if it was true, it was pretty cool that their great-grandfathers had worked on this place together. He tried to dig up any other stories from his memory, stories that had been floating around Blue Lake forever.

"Louis scraped by with the business until the 50s, when he died. Your grandfather was the oldest son, so he inherited. He decided to use it as a family vacation home."

"And my dad continued in that tradition, except that his father willed the property to all his kids together. So dad had to buy his sisters out."

"It's funny you all never did away with the registration counter or the wall shelf for the keys and mail."

"We were a big family, and we always came up here together. So this little table didn't work for meals. We had a big old long table in the office where we ate. We played in there, behind the registration counter. Hung our beach towels on those old key hooks. Right by the door, there was a big basket for our sand toys."

Eva's voice softened and her eyes seemed far away. Daniel knew that after her aunts sold out to Eva's dad, the family never came up again. Not even Eva and her parents. He wondered why, but didn't ask.

The coffee pot gurgled to a halt, pulling her from her memories back into the present with him. She got up to pour two cups.

"Sugar or cream?"

"Just sugar."

She lifted on tiptoe to the top shelf for the bag of sugar, exposing, he could not help but notice, one smooth curvy hip and a dainty indentation of waistline. Before he knew it, he was beside her, one hand on her skin, the other effortlessly snagging the sugar that had been just out of her reach.

Chapter Five

"I don't have a sugar bowl." Of all the things she could have said, this was about the stupidest. But she couldn't help it. His hand on her naked midriff made her an instant idiot.

"I bought all kinds of dishes and treasures for the cottages at the antique store in town," she babbled.

"But not a single sugar bowl," he added.

"Or a creamer."

They stood there at her kitchen counter talking about coffee condiments, and she swore it was turning into the sexiest conversation she'd ever had.

He was so close she could smell the beach on his skin. They moved at the same time, sat across from each other at the little table, sipping coffee. Even though she was famished, the cookies sat on a pretty plate between them untouched. She wasn't hungry for cookies.

"Here's what I was thinking," Daniel said. He had a great voice. He could be on the radio. But what was he talking about? A museum?

"…and we could do a barter. I'll fix your wood, the steps and the registration counter and the window sashes, if you find and furnish period pieces, set up displays in my museum. All on my dime of course. I want the best."

"While you're in Georgia?"

He nodded enthusiastically, a young man ready to set out in search of new horizons. She understood why he would want to spread his wings. She just didn't like it. And if she was honest—the truth embarrassed her—she might not like his bossy attitude when it came to Bryman, but she was attracted to every other single thing about him.

"Sounds like a perfect plan." She injected more happiness into her voice than she felt. "For me."

"Winters up here are brutal. Just leaving your house to check on my places will make it worth my while."

"Okay." Having Daniel do woodwork would save her a bundle. "But it still doesn't seem fair."

"I have more ideas about what you can do for me."

Whoa. Her face turned pink. He couldn't mean what she thought he did.

"Let me document the work we do here at Blue Heaven. Take before and after photos that I can add to my museum collection. I have some old pictures, too. Maybe you do as well? From when your family came up summers?"

"I think so. Well, my mom does. But she can send them to me."

Daniel took a breath. Things were beginning to go his way. "I have a friend at *Discovery Architect.* He knows Bryman, knows me. I'm betting the Blue Heaven restoration will be the thing that finally gets him to write us up. A summer resort on a Great Lake. Perfect."

An illogical tiny corner of disappointment wedged into her heart. He was way more interested in her property than he was in her. But hey, he trusted her with his money. That said something.

****

Daniel's earnestness was winning her over. He'd grabbed her hand across the Formica table and rubbed her palm with his thumb. Did he realize that what he was doing ramped up her attraction to him? She didn't care. His skin against hers felt good. She didn't pull away.

Car doors slammed and engines revved to life. Then within seconds, the air around them was still. Really? Five o'clock already? They'd been talking for hours, but it had seemed like minutes.

"When can I see the rest of the house?"

What was left were the bedrooms, two of which were crammed with boxes of antique store finds for the cottages, and the empty laundry room. Of course he probably wanted to check out her claw-foot tub in the bathroom.

After he'd quickly glanced into the other rooms, they ended up in her favorite room of the house right now. Her bedroom. This was the only room she was really comfortable in. Here were all her things: red laptop, flat screen television, iPod, and docking station. Her big bed from the condo and the white eyelet comforter with matching pillow shams. The weathered oak floor scattered with colorful rag rugs, the Battenberg lace curtains hanging at the window. She'd painted this room herself, before the movers came with her bed. The warm cream-colored walls showed off old brass wall sconces.

"Wow," Daniel said, not paying as much attention as she thought he would to the sconces. He sat on the bed.

"Yeah, a real room." Her heart sped up. He was sitting on her bed. She wanted to walk up to him, put her hands on his chest and push him down onto the mattress.

Her heart beat double time. Triple. She tried to take deep calming breaths. This was ridiculous. He sat innocently on her bed. Looking at her. Not her wall sconces. Not the wavy glass in her window. Her. Right before her eyes, he turned into the Superman she'd wanted him to be. Helping her take her dream to the next level.

"Lovely," he said, and she didn't know if he meant the room or her. The way he gazed into her eyes, as if he could see down to her soul, made her think he was interested in her, not her property.

Daniel got up from the bed and came to her without breaking eye contact. She let him come, couldn't help it, couldn't fight it.

"You are an amazing woman, Eva Delacroix."

She stood rooted to the spot as he approached her, the air between them thick with desire.

"You're pretty great yourself," she answered, her words coming out in a husky whisper.

He was as close as he could get without taking her into his arms, and still he looked at her, not smiling, just holding her gaze. He smelled like the beach. Her eyes fell to his mouth.

Her stomach growled.

They both laughed.

"Hungry?"

She nodded, her eyes closed. She was a little embarrassed. What she was hungry for was his kiss.

As if he could read her mind, Daniel took her in his

arms and kissed her.

Strong arms, soft lips, warm mouth. She could melt into him, she was melting, her thoughts dissolving. Anybody who could kiss like this, so deep and sweet, was worth taking a chance on.

He finally broke the kiss, immediately putting his mouth on her neck and kissing her there, his lips trailing down the V of her blouse.

Her heart roared with need, like thunder. Wait. That *was* thunder. Real thunder. Outside the window.

"The windows are open," she said, reluctant to let anything, even the rain that had started pouring in sheets, interfere with was happening between them.

"I'll close them," he said.

Eva went toward the beach side of the house, while he headed into the office. She was just about to slam the last living room window shut when she heard a baby cry. She listened harder. Another sound, like a crazy woman screeching. As she closed the last window, she saw a big black cat, tail swishing, staring at the weeds next to her door. The cat Bob said lived in her shed.

The cat ignored the rain, slowly heading for the weeds, then backed up screeching when another cat, this one a dirty white with orange splashes, reared up, claws extended, hissing.

Black Cat skulked away and White Cat, looking bedraggled, skinny, and sad, swished her tail while eyeing Eva through the rain-streaked window.

"Oh, honey," Eva said, opening the door, hoping the cat would come in. It retreated into the weeds, where Eva saw the little nest of kittens, tiny as thumbs, curled on a soggy piece of old cardboard.

The kittens had not been there yesterday when

she'd washed the windows. They were so small. Newborns. Thunder clapped and lightning ripped the sky. These babies needed to be warm and dry, now, but when Eva went outside to try to move them, Mama cat bit her hand.

Eva went into the kitchen to wash her hands, thankful that Mama's bite had not broken skin. She'd need to find a vet. Daniel leaned against a wall, talking on his cell. He said a terse good-bye and pocketed his phone.

"All set," he said, indicating the windows. She nodded then opened a can of tuna, flaking it onto a plate.

"Help," she said, when Daniel came up behind her and kissed her neck, his hands holding her tight around her waist, pulling her body close to his. She wasn't sure if she was asking him to help her or asking the universe to help her resist him. She handed Daniel the plate of tuna, which he accepted with a quizzical frown, and went looking for a blanket. She quickly grabbed one from the linen closet and motioned for Daniel to follow her to the living room. She dropped the blanket next to the door and placed the plate of tuna on the porch. Then, while she was still pointing out the kittens to Daniel, Mama rushed to the plate of food.

While Mama ate as if she were starved, Daniel scooped up the kittens, cardboard and all, and plopped them gently onto the blanket inside the house.

Mama was in after them within seconds, hissing at Eva and Daniel and fussing over her babies. The plate on the porch was empty. Eva closed the door and gently pulled the kitten blanket a little further away from the door. Mama licked her babies in between throwing furious looks at Eva and Daniel.

"You're a fierce Mama, aren't you?" Eva spoke softly to the cat. "You're taking really good care of your babies." She looked at Daniel. "Some day, I want to be a mom like that."

Eva, flustered by her admission, went into the kitchen and got Mama a bowl of water and another can of tuna. Before she put it on the plate, Mama came running. She had babies to feed, and to do that, she needed nourishment.

Eva went to check on the kittens. Daniel's big, banged up hands carefully rolled the wet cardboard away as the kittens tumbled together like a big fluff ball onto the warm, dry blanket. Mama came yelling, but somehow she didn't seem quite as fierce with two cans of tuna in her. Soon, the kittens set to nursing; Mama purred with contentment.

"I envy her," Eva said, before she could stop the words from escaping.

"Looks like your first guests have arrived," Daniel said, ignoring, or maybe not hearing, her comment. Eva thought about the black cat still outside, hoping he had a secret entrance to the shed or at least some shelter.

She picked her cell up from the table. "Do you have the number for a vet?"

He took her phone in one hand and his in another, then punched in a number. "Used to go to school with her. She's the best, also the only, vet in town."

"I have to leave." Daniel handed her phone back, already walking toward the office. "There's an emergency at the four-square." His museum. She felt a rush of disappointment. So, they were not going to continue the kissing. She wanted to see where it would lead. But that was probably foolish. He turned around to finish his sentence. "The museum roof is leaking. Bob's over there with Frank." He was leaving. *Get over it.* She stared at the vet's name and number, not really seeing the words or numbers.

"I've got to get into dry clothes," she said.

He smiled, his mind clearly on his Bryman property and not the kiss they'd shared less than ten minutes ago. Or the fact that she'd just mentioned taking off her clothes.

Thunder clapped and Eva shivered. She had kissed Daniel, had agreed to let him help her with the restoration. Maybe those had been wrong decisions. Their priorities were in conflict. His involved working her crew on his own second shift. And moving all the way to Georgia for the winter, while she stayed here alone to freeze.

Chapter Six

At the local grocery store, Eva loaded up with pet supplies and a frozen pizza. In the checkout lane, someone tapped her on the back. Jane had a single item, a tube of toothpaste, in her hand.

"Oh, please, go ahead of me," Eva said.

Jane eyed her cart. "No, that's okay. I just wanted to say hi. I see you've come with pets."

"Other way around, really."

Jane raised an eyebrow but didn't inquire further.

"It's a really good thing I like cats," Eva said, starting to pile her cans of food and a forty pound carton of litter onto the counter.

"That's your dinner?" Jane said, when she unloaded the frozen pizza.

Eva shrugged.

"Why don't we go out to Pointe Lacey? They have a great seafood place right on the pier."

Eva thought about it for a minute. She did owe Jane a bottle of wine. The rain was slowing down and the frozen pizza looked pitiful when she saw it through Jane's eyes.

An hour later, they were seated at a table by the restaurant's window, sipping yet another wonderful bottle of Chardonnay. Eva planned to stick to a single glass, because, one, she wasn't much of a drinker, and two, Jane was, so Eva had offered to drive.

"What are you going to do here in the winter?" Jane asked. "Blue Lake is dead from January until June. And it gets damn cold."

Eva thought about Daniel's offer. Should she tell Jane? What the hell.

"I got an interesting offer," she said.

"Really?" Jane asked. "You're going to stay?"

Eva didn't state the obvious. She really couldn't afford to go elsewhere. Jane would have known that if she'd looked at Eva's business plan. Her projected earnings for the first year would just about cover expenses. She hoped.

"So what's the offer?" Jane picked up the bottle of wine and refilled her glass. She started to pour some for Eva, but noticed her glass was still half full and returned the bottle to the silver cooler at the side of the table.

Eva told Jane about Daniel's barter deal.

"I sense some hesitation on your part," Jane said.

Eva took a drink of her wine. "Should I trust him?"

Jane seemed fascinated. "Why wouldn't you?"

Eva didn't want to get into it, which made the waiter bringing their meals just then perfect. Or so she thought. After a bite of her seafood and pasta, Jane asked again. "Why not trust him?"

Eva finished chewing her bite of steak. It was way better than frozen pizza, but even she knew she should have ordered red wine with it instead of sharing Jane's Chardonnay. Ah well.

"Everything okay, ladies?"

"You know, I'll have a glass of Pinot Noir instead," Eva said. She handed her almost untouched glass to the waiter.

"Good choice," he said, taking away her glass.

Jane looked at the wine as it left the table with obvious dismay, but she didn't say anything. She was still waiting for Eva to explain herself.

Eva hedged. "Well, he didn't want to give me the loan. Then he recommended his brother for my work crew. Hell, he recommended most of my crew. Who he then hired to do second shift at the four-square."

Jane nodded, her eyes going misty.

Eva thought that in light of female solidarity, the least Jane could do was look a little outraged.

"You know Daniel and I used to date," Jane said. "Off and on, ever since high school."

"God. No. I didn't."

"I was like a mother to Bobby. But every time Daniel got to feeling too tied down, he'd break things off. Then a few months later, he'd realize I was the best thing that ever happened to him, and he'd beg me to take him back."

Eva didn't know what to say.

Jane drained her second glass of wine and poured a third, which finished off the bottle.

"Which is why," Jane said, lifting her glass and sipping before finishing her thought, "I agree with you. You shouldn't trust him. He puts Bryman before everything else."

Eva's heart felt as heavy as one of the freighters out on the lake. Heavy and sinking fast. She'd hoped Jane would reassure her about Daniel. Take away her fears. That hadn't happened. She was glad when the waiter returned with her wine. A little bit of something to mellow her mood.

"The truth? He wants what you have. He asked me

dozens of times to pressure your dad, and then even your mom, to sell." Jane got quiet after her admission. Maybe embarrassed that she'd revealed too much to such a new friend. As a Realtor, Jane was being less than discreet, maybe even breaking some kind of Realtor code. But Eva was glad to know Daniel's interest in her was far from pure. She was glad to have this warning to guard her heart. Eva knew how to fix Jane's silent brooding, too. When one woman shares a hurt from her past, the other follows with a piece of her own sad love history.

"I dated this guy for six years," Eva admitted. "He was my boss. I started at the agency when I got out of high school. I was just a secretary and he was a big shot. He was older. He taught me a lot, and eventually we started an affair. It didn't end well."

"Men can be such pigs." Jane reached for the wine bottle, noticed it was empty, and held it up, swishing it back and forth until the waiter noticed.

Chapter Seven

The next morning, as Eva searched for the black cat so the vet who'd come out to check over Mama and the kittens could look at him too, Daniel showed up along with Bob, Frank, and the rest of the crew. Eva had been half expecting nobody to show, had been picturing them at the museum. She decided to trust Daniel, if not with her heart, then at least with her beach steps. He was, after all, working for free. And he knew that she was never going to sell, no matter what.

Daniel said hi on his way down to the beach. She waved and plastered what she hoped was a casual smile onto her face. After Jane's revelations last night, she was glad he was here, but also in high alert mode.

"Looking for something?" Bob asked.

"Black cat," she said, peered under some shrubbery.

"You check the shed?"

"Yes."

"He hangs out in the rafters," Bob said, before excusing himself to get the crew organized for the day.

Eva went back to the shed while the vet waited on the stoop. She didn't seem to mind sitting on a slab of concrete, but Eva wanted a beautiful front porch for guests. She could picture the overhang from the addition, stone piers, sturdy wicker furniture, bright pillows, slate floor.

"Yeow." She heard him before she saw him, peering at her from above.

"Hi there Daddy. Your wife and babies are fine." He gave a lower pitched meow that sounded more like a grunt.

"He's in here, doc." The vet came into the shed with her bribe. The two of them had a staring contest for a minute with the cat.

"Why don't I go up there," Eva was already climbing a ladder, "and I'll chase him down, then you can nab him."

The vet and Eva stood ready as the cat elegantly exited the rafter for the floor below without the help of anything so mundane as a step ladder. His furry descent was the stuff of Olympic gold. He landed at the doc's feet, scarfing the piece of cooked chicken she held out to him.

In a matter of seconds, the doc bagged the cat with a blanket, gripped him firmly despite his outraged howls, and got him out of the shed and into her mobile unit.

Eva stood on the ladder, looking around the rough attic space. This was the final frontier, the last little spot she hadn't investigated on her property. There wasn't much to see. A couple of dusty boxes and a long piece of PVC pipe. Or maybe, she thought, reaching out for it, a cylinder poster container. She pulled at it. Not heavy. With black daddy cat patrolling the rafters, she was pretty sure there wouldn't be any mice lurking inside. Maybe spiders. She could handle those.

She grabbed the awkwardly-sized tube around the middle and slowly stepped down the ladder. Whatever it contained, the tube was cardboard, not plastic. Bob had set up a worktable from two sawhorses and a plank of plywood, so she maneuvered the tube onto the table and opened the capped end. Looked like a poster inside. She carefully pulled it out, not having a clue what relic she'd find. Her aunts had cleaned out most of the family heirlooms, claiming the china and linens her dad hadn't cared about. But apparently, he'd salvaged something, and tucked it here not too long ago by the good condition of the paper. She unrolled the heavy spool and knew what it was.

Not stocks and bonds, not even a Woodstock poster, but the original blueprints for the bungalow. Or somebody's bungalow. Because, unlike Blue Heaven, these blueprints showed a second floor, airplane style, with the gorgeous big porch of her dad's dreams looking out to the lake. But there was the name, Blue Heaven, in the right bottom corner. And Bryman's name. And her great-grandfather's, along with the date in 1922 when the house was built.

What had happened? Why hadn't the second floor ever materialized? She went back up the ladder and retrieved the boxes. There were just two, and they were fairly small and light. Before she could open them, the vet came back with a purring daddy cat, which she confirmed was indeed a male. About four years old, and in good health.

"Are they..." Eva didn't know the term for wild, dangerous, unfriendly.

"Not feral, no. They're domesticated. Probably got lost or someone turned them out. Happens all the time."

Eva didn't like to think about the kind of people who would simply tire of their pet and not let them back into the house one night.

They settled the bill inside the bungalow, leaving Daddy to rearrange himself in his quarters. As Eva watched the vet drive away, she heard man noises from the shed.

"What the hell? I can't believe—"

She rushed outside to the shed. Bob and Daniel were at the worktable pouring over the blueprints.

"Do you still think I shouldn't add a second story?"

Daniel studied the blueprints. "Where'd you find these?"

"Up there." She pointed to the rafters. "And these boxes, too," she said, prying open the first box. "Letters," she said.

Bob and Daniel came up beside her. "From my grandfather to yours. And from yours to mine." Eva picked up yellowed envelope after yellowed envelope, most still with the penny stamp in the upper right corner. She flipped open the other box.

"And preliminary drawings, there, looks like," Daniel said. He still hadn't snatched or even touched anything from the boxes, even though some of the letters were rightly his property. How had her father come to own both sides of the correspondence? Maybe the letters themselves would tell the story.

****

A gust of wind stirred the air, and one of the letters almost flew out of the box.

"We need to take these inside," Daniel said.

"Yes." He was bossy, but he was also right. Bob went back to work and Eva and Daniel went into her bungalow. They sat on the living room floor and spread out letters, photos, and even receipts, a collage of history. At the center, weighed down with salt and pepper shakers, was the blue print.

Eva looked at a receipt for a pound of nails. "Do they still sell nails by the pound?"

Daniel had been studying the wedding photograph of his great-grandparents. He looked up and she saw his sad eyes. "What? Sorry. Great-grandma looks just like my mom did at that age."

She held out her hand for the picture. They exchanged the pieces of history and he laughed at the receipt, ten cents for one pounds of nails. "She was so pretty," Eva said.

"She was," Daniel agreed. Eva wasn't sure which "she" he meant, but it didn't really matter.

They worked together, sorting the mementos into two piles of pictures, two piles of letters, and a pile of miscellaneous papers, like the receipt for nails. Daniel would keep his letters and photos, and she would keep hers.

After they'd filed the letters by date, they moved to the sofa, each with a pile of letters in their laps. The envelope glue was gone, the ink on the old pages had faded, the creases were browned with age, but the words told the story of a friendship that developed over time, about a world long gone, where soup lines in Detroit delivered many people's only meal of the day. In Blue Lake, hunting and fishing were not sports, they were survival skills. Both great-grandmothers had gardens and took great pride in "putting up" jars of peaches and green beans. A few of the letters shared recipes written on small cards, in different hands, those of two wives doing their part to wrestle a living off the land.

And it was in the letters that a plan was hatched

between the two men to change the course of Blue Heaven from a summer retreat into a new means of making money for the Delacroix family. In one letter, Daniel found a rough sketch of the cottages. He handed it to her. "No gloating."

She just smiled. At last they could share her vision.

After they'd looked through everything, they got up to stretch and realized it was dusk. Too late to start on the beach stairs.

"It feels wrong to break up this collection," Daniel said. "It's on your property, so I guess you have first claim."

"No, you should have your letters and photos. Anyway, there's so much mess and confusion going on here. I think everything will be better kept at your place for now."

"We need copies of the blueprint. I know a guy in Port Huron who does specialized copying. Nobody should handle this original."

Eva carefully rolled the blueprint up and put it back into the cylinder. "I'll take it in to him tomorrow."

"I'll call to let him know you're coming and what you have."

"Maybe I'll frame the original and hang it in the office."

Daniel's face fell. "That would be nice," he said, making an effort. *Oh. He probably would love that blueprint for his museum.*

After they'd labeled and sorted everything and organized them into boxes on the kitchen table, Daniel said "There's no way we can stay in your budget now that we have these blueprints."

Eva tensed. "Hold on." Sure, their ancestors had

worked together. Sure, they could, too. But this was her project, and Daniel, no matter his many skills and considerable charm, would work on her budget and within her timetable.

"William Bryman and Louis Delacroix lived in times quite similar to ours," she told Daniel, trying to hold a reasonable tone even as her hands curled into fists and arranged themselves on her hips. "When the Depression hit, and Louis decided to change course, William went along with him. They built cottages and modified the bungalow. They bought linoleum instead of wood, they used cheaper products without sacrificing quality. They made deliberate decisions to maximize the earning potential for this place. Which is what I am doing." She let her arms fall loosely around her body, trying hard to smooth out this dispute. Every time she saw Daniel, she liked him a little more. She didn't want their shared history, and his intense focus on it, to make them awkward around each other.

"But to be the best..."

"I hear you. I do. Quality counts. Except you have piles of money, and I don't."

"I'm happy to loan you whatever you need. And I won't charge you interest. You don't ever have to pay me back. Once this place gets into *Discovery Architecture...*" Daniel had been talking all morning about how his writer friend would not be able to resist this new angle of a renovated beach resort. "...you will never have to advertise again. You will be able to raise your rates. You will be able to show off your showplace."

Eva rubbed her bare arms. She felt raw. Maybe it was the sun going down, or maybe it was her past come back to haunt her. On the one hand, she knew the kind of advertising Daniel was talking about could not be bought, not on her budget. On the other, she'd been through this before. A wealthy successful man saw a way to exploit her by helping her along the path to success. Dangerous, complicated success.

"Let me take you to dinner. We can talk about it over one of Eddie's burgers." Daniel said.

"No, I…listen Daniel, I have some work to do. Calls to make. A marketing campaign to write. I appreciate you working the magazine angle, and I'll help all I can if it pans out, but right now I need to find paying customers."

He looked hurt. Part of her melted and part of her steeled herself against giving in. Marcus had been able to manipulate her emotions, but that was the past. This was now. She wouldn't let Daniel do it, too.

"But what about my offer of a loan? Please don't turn me down. This property is too important now to use second rate materials or workers."

She shook her head.

"I'm sorry, Daniel. I'm sure your offer is sincere." She wasn't, not quite, but he didn't have to know that. "It's just—I have to do this my way. Within my budget." She always had the 401K to tap into if she needed it.

Chapter Eight

When the roofer finished shingling the cottages, he told her he had a builder—a great builder, he claimed—to help with the airplane addition. After running the numbers again, Eva cashed out her anemic 401k. It was the only way she could afford to pay all these people and buy materials.

Eva showed them the fragile blueprints, making sure no one touched them. "I'll get you a set to work with later."

"We can have it boxed in and roofed in two week's time," the builder promised. "Then it's just a matter of finish work."

Five weeks until opening. It might just be enough time. And if not, well, that would be fine. Daniel had been right about the cottages being first priority. As soon as these two built a staircase and got the addition buttoned up, she could finish the office and be ready for business, even if the upper floor wasn't completely finished.

"Might have to give me one or two more guys off the cottage crew," Frank said.

That could be a problem.

"I need a cottage to live in while the bungalow is roofless, so I'm not sure who Bob can spare."

"We'll work it out," Frank promised.

Eva hoped they could. And she hoped Daniel

would not get in the way. He'd already talked her into having copies made of the blueprints so that nobody else handled the originals. Even though she wanted to have them framed and put in her office, she was sure he wanted them for his museum.

She had to drive all the way to Port Huron to get the printing job done, and when she returned, it was after five. Bob gave her some good news.

"Three of the cottages are just about livable."

"Just about?"

"The interior of Peach is complete." Peach is where Eva planned to set up headquarters for her publicity campaign. They walked over, Eva soothed and satisfied at the busy construction scene. Men moving with purpose, hammers pounding out a righteous ring, lumber hoisted on responsible shoulders, all coordinated like a testosterone ballet. And Peach! Great bones. She needed to decorate. Set the stage for photos. For her, that was the fun part of doing publicity.

"The other two are coming along, but need a bit more work," Bob said. Eva really didn't care about the other two cottages. Progress was being made, things were moving on schedule, maybe even a little bit ahead of time.

"Is my wireless going to work out here?" She needed to nail marketing while construction went on around her.

"No problem." She noted that a single bed she'd stored in the spare room had been moved into Peach.

Now she just had to carry the kittens over.

Bob followed Eva into the house. The builder and roofer had made a rough start in the office on the winding stairway. At least she hoped it was a rough start, because what they had nailed up as steps looked worse than the old ones down at the beach. Maybe it wasn't the best of ideas to hire a roofer and an unknown person to erect an addition. But Frank had sworn he'd done plenty of construction besides roofing and that his builder buddy was as good as they came. As she checked out the sorry steps, and a slice of sky above, a girl in shorts and a crop top came in to the office without knocking.

"There's no toilet paper in my cottage," she told Bob, ignoring Eva. "And it smells like mildew."

Bob blushed. He looked from the girl to Eva.

"I sort of rented out one of the cottages," Bob shrugged, not looking Eva in the eye but casting his baby blues out to the lake as if watching for whales.

"Are you the owner?" The girl addressed Eva. "Because I need some toilet paper. And you," she pointed to Bob, "have got to open my window. It's painted shut."

"I don't have a business license yet," Eva told Bob. "So, I can't rent you a room," she told the girl.

"I can't pay for the room anyway," the girl said, "so you're not really renting it to me per se." She held out her hand. "Lily Van Styke."

Eva shook Lily's perfectly manicured hand.

Bob went into the bathroom and came out holding out a roll of toilet paper to Lily.

"Lily's going to help us paint," Bob said.

Bob hiring another crew member was fine, but only if he paid her out of the budget she'd already provided him. Lily staying in one of the cottages wasn't a good idea. She started to say as much when Lily interrupted her.

"Where are the sheets?" Lily walked through the kitchen and into the hallway to rummage through the linen closet. Eva didn't even have a washing machine yet, let alone proper linens. She'd need them soon. Another trip to Port Huron was on the horizon. But not today. Today she'd get Peach ready to occupy and move in. Her website was just waiting for photos and a few final bits of code. She wanted it up and running tonight as well. But what to do about this girl?

"This is not going to work. I'm not set up for you," Eva said, wondering how much credit she still had on her Sears card. She really should arrange delivery of a heavy duty washer and dryer.

"These will do, for now," Lily said, coming out with Eva's second set of queen-sized sheets.

"You don't even have a bed," Eva said.

Bob shrugged. "I gave her one from my house. We have so many bedrooms nobody uses, Daniel will never even notice." He turned to Lily. "Those sheets should work fine."

Lily sat down, plunking her roll of toilet paper on the chair next to her. "And you need mousetraps."

They both ignored Eva's remark about Lily not staying. It was as if she hadn't spoken.

"Forget the mousetraps. I've got a cat with kittens," Eva said. "They're just a bit too small to start working for their keep yet." The same could be said of Lily. "I'm sorry, Lily, but the cottages aren't ready to be lived in."

Lily shot off the chair. "Kittens! Where?"

Eva pointed to the living room. Bob followed Lily and Eva trailed after them, wondering what she could do to get rid of this girl who seemed oblivious to Eva's strong hints that she had to go.

"God, this room is gorgeous." In spite of herself, Eva warmed incrementally toward Lily. She'd loved decorating her living room even though she'd maxed out her Visa to do it.

A squeal indicated Lily had spied the kittens. "Awwww."

Eva didn't know how to contain this exuberant woman-child, so instead she scratched a purring Mama cat under the chin. Cats were easy. A baby would be easy compared to this teenager. Eva and Marcus were supposed to be starting their family now. She had wanted it, had pushed for it. Maybe too hard. He'd backed off, backed out of everything. Never mind. For now what she had were baby kittens and, apparently, a human teenager.

"They're still too small to handle," Lily said, when Bob reached out to touch a kitten. Eva wondered if Lily had been raised on a farm, or at least a place big enough for barn cats. She hadn't seen any vehicle except Bob's truck in the driveway. So either Lily had walked here or someone had dropped her off. Or, God forbid, she'd been hitch-hiking on the highway.

After the proper amount of admiration for the kittens, Lily walked back out to the kitchen. Bob and Eva followed. Lily picked up her toilet paper, stabbing Bob with a powerful gaze.

"The window. Right," he said. "Be right there."

He rummaged in a bag laying on the table, dumping the contents, a dozen mousetraps, onto the table. He snagged one and started after Lily.

"Bob," Eva said, "Lily looks awfully young."

"She is, but that's okay," Bob said. "Since I'm

staying in the cabin next to her, she should be safe. And since you're giving us room and board, I can fit her into the budget you've given me."

"You're moving in?" That meant he'd be onsite full time. Probably not a bad idea, but still, Eva was astounded. "You live with Daniel."

"Yeah, I did. I had to move out. He was giving me grief."

"Why?" Eva remembered back to her days as an eighteen year old. Grief covered a lot of territory. Like everything. Eva's head pounded. She couldn't turn these kids away. Not right now. Not unless she wanted Lily hitchhiking further downstate to her possible death by serial killer who preyed on young female hitchhikers.

"Didn't you say the bathrooms in those cabins are still non-functional?" Eva asked.

"They're okay. I turned the water on and my toilet and sink work. We can just use your bathroom to shower and stuff."

Eva hoped he didn't mean her cottage bathroom. Those places were tiny. She had to draw the line somewhere, inexperienced as she was at doing so. "Listen, Bob, you and Lily can use the bungalow bathroom, but not my cottage. I will be working round the clock and cannot be disturbed."

"That's cool."

"How old is Lily?"

"Eighteen," Bob said. "I checked her I.D."

If Lily had been on the road, she was probably hungry. And if Bob was actually living here, he'd be hungry by dinnertime, too. Didn't young men eat their equivalent in body weight on a daily basis? Her cupboard was bare. Eva felt baffled at suddenly finding herself surrounded by kids and cats, not to mention the promise of enormous grocery bills. At least for a little while. Until Eva could discover Lily's story and figure out how to get her home where she belonged.

"Lily would be a great maid, you know, once you get the cottages renting." Bob, obviously sensing her reservations about the situation, had followed Eva out to the office.

She had been planning to hire a woman to assist her. It was hard enough keeping her own house clean without doing it six more times every week. The laundry. The vacuuming. With the lake, the towels alone would be a nightmare. And Lily could help her with so many little things, like washing the china and other stuff for the cottages. Eva had what felt like an endless list of stuff that needed doing, stuff that took time away from her working on the marketing campaign, which had to be, for the next several days, her top priority.

What she really needed now, this minute, was to talk to someone who could advise her on how to handle teenagers. She only knew one person in Blue Lake who fit that bill. And he probably wasn't going to be happy that one of the teenagers she needed help with was his little brother.

Chapter Nine

Eva drove through town, riding up and down streets, looking for Daniel's house. She wasn't sure how he was going to take the news that Bob was moving in with her. Or that she had hired a pair of guys to do a job that they, by the look of the staircase they'd started, didn't seem equipped to handle.

She parked in front of Daniel's house. Okay, she could do this. She could ask for his advice without crossing any lines. They could be friends. They could work together. They didn't have to go any further than that. Yes, she was attracted to him, but that was just left-over baby lust from Marcus. Or maybe seeing Mama with her kittens had brought that subliminal desire for a baby roaring back to life, and her cavewoman genes had chosen Daniel for the daddy. That was all this was. But she was smarter than biology. And stronger.

She stared at the huge house. It sat upon a good amount of space on the wide lot. Three-storied. Brick. Large porch with the thick stone piers. She was stalling. How to ask for his help? How to bring up the subject? "Oh by the way, your brother took some beds from your house and moved in with me and a teenage girl he picked up off the highway" seemed inappropriate on so many levels. She wouldn't mention the roof situation, the attempt at a staircase, or that scary sliver of sky. For all she knew, they'd just roughed something in to get an idea of dimension. They'd probably be fine once they got into it. Okay, she needed to quit stalling and just go ring the doorbell already.

She climbed, trepidation and something else, possibly house envy, in every step. The details of this house were perfect. Mellow warm brick. Wood trim stained a gorgeous mahogany color. Gleaming glass inserts in double front doors. Thanks to Daniel, she now knew that this glass was original, knew how to spot the waviness that gave it away. And she was still stalling. What was he going to do, bite her? And why did that random thought make her heart pound harder?

She took a breath and rang the bell. She heard footsteps and then there was Daniel, at the door. Looking too beautiful to be a bad guy. If it ever happened, if they did have a child together, it would be a beauty. Male or female. Just with his DNA alone. *Stop it!* she warned herself.

"Hey you, come on in." He seemed delighted to see her.

"I don't want to disturb you, but something's come up."

"With Blue Heaven?"

She wanted to confide in him about her doubts regarding her building team, but resisted. "No, the project's fine."

"Oh. Good."

Gee, she felt like an idiot. She suddenly blanked on why she was here.

"How's it going? What do you need?" He took both her hands and pulled her from the porch into an entryway as big as her bedroom.

****

When Eva had shown up at Daniel's door, it was as if he'd conjured her. He'd just been thinking about her, daydreaming about the way her stomach curved in and how those curves were places you could get lost in. They'd gotten close to something the other day at her place. Maybe today they would get back there, and then some.

"Want a quick tour?" He'd like to start the tour in the bedroom, but that would be too obvious. In some ways, Eva seemed as skittish as her cat.

"Well, okay." Something was on her mind, but it couldn't be too important or she'd have said what it was by now. Probably wanted to take him up on his loan offer and didn't know how to ask.

He would put her at ease with his Bryman chat.

"This is the first house Bryman designed. And a member of his family has lived in it ever since."

He led her through the dining room and into the kitchen. The three rooms were large, with wide openings. He pointed out features without really paying attention to his words. He couldn't even hear himself, so focused was he on her standing next to him. He wanted to take her in his arms and do it on the dining room table. Even if she let him, and that was a big IF, it would probably be a mistake. Take it slow, that was the ticket.

"Scullery, laundry room, servant's dining room, which I use as my office. I've kept everything authentic."

In the other wing, he pointed out his billiard room, a library, and a room his mother had always called a morning room, maybe because it got full sun at that time of day.

"My grandmother liked to sew in here," he said. She walked into every room, touching fabric, looking closely at wallpaper patterns, running her hands over the clean lines of the polished period furniture. She had run her hands over his skin, in just that same slow way.

He led her to his bedroom door. Sure, he'd skipped the four bathrooms and the other bedrooms. There were seven in all, and he didn't have that kind of patience just now. Even though the stairs were right next to his rooms, he didn't take her up to the third floor where the servant's rooms used to be.

They stood rooted to the spot in front of his bedroom door.

"And this is the master suite," he said, throwing open the door, pulling her inside, showing her how two bedrooms connected through the closet.

"There's enough room for a bed in this closet," she said. She'd been strangely silent through the tour. Some people got that way when they saw the house. It really was a grand old place. Daniel was very proud of it. He wasn't trying to flaunt his wealth. He loved this old pile of stones, not because it was a status symbol, but because it was his heritage.

"I'm overwhelmed."

"There was something you wanted to tell me," he said, confident she'd come about the loan. He hoped she wouldn't think she had to sleep with him to get the money. "If it's about the loan, my offer still stands."

"No, it's not that." She seemed to be fighting an internal war, trying to figure out what to say or how to say it and saying nothing instead. So he kissed her.

Chapter Ten

Eva wanted, more than anything, to feel Daniel's mouth on hers. His kiss deepened and her cautious thoughts swam away like little fishes. She didn't care. The sweetest thing, more than burning, more than desire, was feeling this close, like she knew him down to her soul, or at least his kiss knew the primal spot sweet and low inside her, where she ached to connect with him.

In his arms, she was not unemployed, not in over her head, not a used and discarded thing. There was just now, here, in this bed that felt like it was made of clouds. And him. This man, his hands reaching up under her shirt to feel her skin, resting his hand for a tantalizing moment against her hopeful beating heart before sliding them slowly down her breasts and out of her shirt again. *Come back!* She wanted to moan, but then he began pulling her blouse buttons open and kissing her neck. She shivered.

He pulled away just a little bit and looked at her. "Cold?"

"No." She pulled him back to her.

"Good."

And it was. She needed someone. She'd pretended for a long time that she was done with men, but that was just her getting over Marcus. Time to start again. In every way. And she needed to start clean by telling

Daniel what she'd come here to say.

She moved her lips from his, down to his shoulder, putting both hands on either of his hard biceps. He still reached for her when she spoke. "I'm not sure how this started," she said, feeling embarrassed as he finally realized she wanted to talk instead of kiss. He lay there, his eyes smoldering and sexy, taking in every inch of her all unbuttoned and open. "I came over here to talk to you."

"I like this better." He moved closer, closed his eyes.

"No, really. I think I better say this before we go any further. You might get mad at me if I don't tell you."

"Nothing could do that."

He said it, but she could see the gears turning in his mind. He was wondering if she'd blown it with the bungalow somehow. And maybe she did. But that wasn't what she was here to say. Because really, she didn't know those guys were bad at their jobs. She'd give them a little more time. And family was more important anyway.

"Tell me." He took her into his arms and she put her head on his shoulder.

"I wanted to let you know that the roofer brought the builder over today and they made a start on the staircase to the second floor."

Daniel had been kissing her temple, her eyelid, her cheek, but his lips froze in place at her words. He stopped kissing her, eased away a little bit, and listened.

"I showed them the blueprints, but they did not handle them. Nobody's handled the originals but us. I told them I'd get them a set to work off of soon. And then I went to Port Huron and got the copies made."

He took his arms away from her and lay face up on his pillows. She peeked up to see his reaction. His eyes were closed and he was quiet, but he nodded.

"What's the builder's name?"

"Sam something. I have his card in my purse." She had no idea where she'd left her purse. Daniel didn't move when she said the builder's name, but she felt a gap widen between them. He was not happy, but neither was he going to put up a fight. He was going to let her do things her way. Now was probably not the perfect time to tell him the other news, but she felt she should. He had to know. "And Bob moved in."

"What?" His head shot up from the pillows, he frowned at her, then got up from the bed, pacing the floor. She felt stupid on the bed alone so she got up on the other side. He continued pacing as she twisted the buttons of her shirt closed. She could tell from his pacing that he was not happy right now. Not one bit.

"He found this girl hitchhiking on the highway, and he moved her into a cottage and then took another one next to her. They didn't ask me, they did the whole thing while I was getting the blueprints copied in Port Huron. He said he could oversee the cottage renovations better if he stayed on site."

"So send him home."

"I tried that already. I told them the cottages weren't ready, that I wasn't set up yet for other people living on the premises, that I didn't have the cash to pay a maid. They stonewalled me every time. I had no idea teenagers could be so stubborn."

"Welcome to my world."

"So what else can I do?"

"Fire him."

"I can't! I need him. He's working wonders on my cottages. They'll be finished in another week or so."

Daniel shook his head.

"Those cottages aren't near ready for occupation yet!"

"I know. That's what I thought, but Peach is all set; I checked it out before I came here. And Bob claims he's got two more that'll do for now. Apparently he outfitted them with beds and things from the rooms here."

Daniel struggled to get his emotions under control. What they were exactly, she couldn't say. So she guessed.

"You've been a father to Bob all these years. This must be so difficult. Or, maybe, is it the furniture?"

"It's not the furniture," he said. "I did the best I could, but apparently, it wasn't good enough. I mean, he's leaving in the fall anyway. Maybe I should just let him go."

Great. Now the problem of what to do with the teenagers was back in her lap. She didn't see a way out. "I am so not equipped for this."

"It was the same for me. Not a choice. The situation was forced on me. Parenthood at twenty. I wasn't ready for it. Maybe you never are."

But she had been ready to have children with Marcus, who had grown children and had not been interested in starting a second family. Of course he hadn't told her that. For years he'd let her believe in the possibility, listening to her talk about kids and family with an indulgent, pleasant look on his face. When pressed, he'd even say the word "someday" when she'd ask if he could see them having children together. Liar.

Eva and Daniel looked at each other over opposite sides of the bed. Something had almost happened here. Just minutes ago she would have sworn they had started a relationship. And maybe they still could. Maybe he'd stop pacing and start kissing again soon.

"My parenting days are almost over anyway." He stopped pacing at the door to the bedroom. "So in a way, it's a relief." He started walking out of the room. She had no choice but to follow him down the stairs. Kissing over for now.

He stood at the massive front doors. Time for her to leave. "I love Bob," he said, "and I don't regret quitting school to raise him, but I'm so done being a dad."

She sucked her breath in hard. His parenting days were over? As good as Daniel's kisses felt, as fine and gentle as his hands had been on her skin, she had to stop this thing that had hardly gotten started. For her own sake.

Her mother had told her that life was like school, and if you didn't learn your lesson the first time something went wrong, the world would just keep sending you the same lesson in a different situation. That felt exactly what was happening here. Same situation, different guise. And she'd learned her lesson well.

"By the way, Sam's the town drunk."

"What? Who?"

"Sam. Your builder. He's the town drunk. He's okay on a crew, at least until lunch, but he can't do this himself. And a roofer won't know how to cope with building your precious addition."

That stung. She stood at the door, feeling as if he'd just slapped her. He opened one of the wide wood doors, saying *get out* without using any words. He didn't know this, but inside, she was having mini-meltdown. First he'd gotten her into bed way too easily, and then shut off the love the minute he learned about the events of the day, as if everything was her fault. Okay, well the builder was her fault. But not Bob. That was in no way her fault or responsibility. She'd tried to tell him to go home. And right now, she was holding on to too many strands, every single one of them pulling at her, making her temples pound.

"I'll just have to keep an eye on him." She picked up her purse from where she'd dropped it on a table, doing her best to shake off her restless sadness. "I have to go. There's still so much to do."

"I don't see how you're going to have things ready by Memorial Day weekend."

She started to walk away, but his words stopped her.

"I'll have everything done. Don't worry about me."

Of course, the irony was that he wasn't worried about her at all. He was worried about his precious Bryman legacy. And he'd dumped the problem of what to do with Bob and Lily right into her arms.

Chapter Eleven

The next morning, Eva came home after running around dealing with permits and licensing. When she pulled into Blue Heaven the driveway was empty of every vehicle except Bob's truck. *Where had her crew gone?* It was two in the afternoon. They had better not be at Daniel's museum.

Bob and Lily sat sunning themselves on old metal lawn chairs that had been stored in the shed for decades. They both had cans of beer in hand.

"Hello? You two are underage. Give me those!" she pulled the beers from their hands and poured them out on the still straw-like lawn. She didn't like being a parent. It felt mean and bossy.

"Sorry. Sam gave them to us. Said it was about to rain, so the crew called it a day. We can't paint exteriors in the rain."

Eva scanned the lake. There were some black clouds scutting in the distance. "When did Sam start drinking today?"

"Well, he brought a case of beer at noon. It's Friday. That's sort of normal."

Bob had the good grace to look sheepish.

"It's not like we've never had a beer in our life," Lily said. Eva noticed Lily was wearing her favorite hoodie. Cashmere. Lily noticed Eva notice.

"Oh, this. Sorry. I didn't pack enough stuff. Hope

it's okay."

"What? That you borrow my stuff or that you go into my bedroom, into my closet, without permission?" Eva was getting the hang of this parental thing. It had been easier to call Lily on the cashmere than the beer.

Then she noticed the roof. Or rather the absence of one. A flimsy piece of plastic flapped in the wind. It wouldn't stop a teardrop let alone a rainstorm.

"My brother came by," Bob said. Eva's eyes stayed trained on her roofline. At least they'd only taken a piece of it off.

"Did he see this?" She pointed to the place where her roof used to be.

"Yeah. He was so angry about it he fired Sam."

"What?" Eva couldn't believe even Daniel would have the nerve to do that. As bossy as he was, he had to know this was her house, her project, her future. Not his.

"It's okay," Bob said. "He put the fear of God into Sam because of the drinking. Told Sam he was on probation. Told him he couldn't work after drinking. Ever. And sent him home."

"And you didn't think to call me."

"I figured it was handled. I'd have done the same thing myself, but they sort of don't really listen to me. They call me 'Young Blood' and just do things the way they want. Which is usually the right way. Maybe except for the beer."

"I won't leave again while the work is going on," Eva said.

"No offense, but they won't take you much more seriously than they do me. Now Daniel, they'll listen to him."

At that moment, before Eva could fully process that *her crew* would not listen to her, did not, apparently, respect her, Daniel pulled up in his truck, the back loaded down with plywood, tarp, and canvas. He and Bob started unloading immediately.

"I know what you're thinking." Daniel talked as he carried supplies past her. "But it had to be done. And now Bob and I have to get this temporary roof on before the rain starts, so please don't pick a fight. Not now."

Even as he spoke, Eva felt a sprinkle on her face. She didn't say a word, just left them to it. Somehow the idea of her house being open to the elements made her earlier problem of the giant insurance payment from the morning's mail seem not so huge. The budget was tight, but she'd pay her bills. She'd be fine financially. And if Daniel and Bob had anything to say about it, her house wouldn't get too wet in the process. As she thought this, a larger drop splashed across her nose, and then another one.

Two more trucks pulled in just then, a couple crew members jumped out and hustled over to the ladders, climbing to the roof. Eva felt a little better as she watched them work at closing up the gap in her roof, even as the rain started to pour in earnest.

****

They'd secured the house, just in time. Things could have been a lot worse, would have been, without Daniel. Bob and Lily watched local news in the living room, which for now still had an actual roof.

Daniel wiped his tools dry with a rag at the kitchen sink, then put each carefully into an ancient toolbox.

"Thank you," she said. He might not meet all the

requirements of her dream lover, well, he met them all but one. The most important one. Still, he was a good guy. Not his fault he was tired of being tied down. Done being a dad.

"You're welcome."

"I hear you fired Sam."

"I hear you gave my brother beer."

She sighed. "You and I both know that was Sam." But because he'd been so kind, she didn't want to argue. "I'm having a glass of wine. Want one?"

"Sure," he said.

She took two glasses from the cabinet, opened the bottle, and poured.

The weather report came on, and since Bob and Lily were sprawled on the sofa, Eva went over to her little nook with the two cozy chairs by the windows overlooking the lake. She turned on the stained glass lamp, its pool of light reflecting in the windows.

Daniel sat next to her, checking out the room. "You've got a good eye."

"Thanks," she said. His house had felt a little austere. Bryman was a product of the Arts and Crafts period, he liked built-ins and clean lines. Daniel's house reflected all that was most cold and comfortless about the style, at least in Eva's view. She liked built-ins and clean lines just fine, but also warmth, texture, color.

"I hope that girl is really eighteen." Daniel studied Lily.

Eva sipped her wine, looked toward Bob and Lily, their feet tangled together on the fat velvet ottoman.

"I checked her license," Eva said. "She's legal." They sat quietly for awhile. It was so peaceful not to hear the sounds of construction. She could hear the roar of waves and the patter of hard rain falling.

Life was good. Almost perfect. The problem was that she needed Daniel and he knew it. Needed him as her crew foreman, as her builder, not as her lover. The problem was obvious. She had to see him every day and keep her hands—and her lips—to herself.

"You can have the original blueprints and the photos and letters and things for the museum. I'm having the blueprints framed with archival materials. Your friend from the shelter magazine sent an email to tell me about that. So I guess I'm already starting on the museum." She smiled. *Stop babbling.*

"Thank you," he said. "But I will only accept the blueprints if you let me oversee this project."

Her relief was huge. "Yes, please. As long as we can still do a barter. You do this for me, and I put your museum together this winter."

"It will be a labor of love, believe me."

For a minute, Eva's heart skipped. Love for her? But then she quickly realized it was love for all things Bryman.

"So you're done at the bank?"

"Just about." Daniel sipped his wine and smiled a little half smile. "I don't know if this is a coincidence or what, but my life has been changing dramatically since you've come to town. My empty nest. That's weird. And the job at the bank. I've only been part owner since the crash. Old man Augustine needed an investor, so I took it on. Better me than Bank of America, right?"

"So practically your last order of business there was to try to block my loan."

"Busted," he said, finishing off his glass of wine and standing up. "I knew you were the new owner of

Blue Heaven and I had to see what you were up to with the property. It's my…"

"I know," Eva interrupted, getting up as well. "Your heritage."

Chapter Twelve

That night, after Daniel went home and Bob and Lily left for their cottages, Eva moved the rest of her things into Peach, styled for a photo shoot. Lily had swiped Mama and the kittens, who she said would just get in Eva's way.

The cottages consisted of one big room, with big being a relative term. Three tiny areas for sleeping, eating, and living. The bathroom was too small to hold a tub and even the shower stall was dinky, but it was cozy and clean.

She plugged in her phone, iPod, and laptop. Then she took a shower, missing her bathtub with an ache that made her feel weepy and silly. By the time she got to bed, it was already morning. She didn't sleep much and popped up with the sun, which, as the weatherman promised, dawned bright and shiny, quickly burning off the dew and drying up the mud puddles outside.

She flung open the curtains, turned on a few lights, and snapped some interior shots. She opened the door to get more natural light and a wider shot, only to see Daniel standing there. He ignored her surprise and kissed her right on the lips, in front of Bob and Frank, and who knows who else. She wasn't sure, because she pulled Daniel quickly inside and shut the door without checking who had seen what.

"Cozy," he said, scanning the room but keeping

both his arms tight around her waist. She took his hands and gently pried them from her body. Then she dropped his hands and moved back a step.

"Listen, Daniel. If this is going to work—if you and I are going to work together—we need to…" She wasn't sure how to put it. "Be professional. And not kiss. Or anything."

"Oh." He seemed surprised. "What about at my house? And in your bedroom? Something's happening between us. How can you erase it? Because I sure can't."

"It was nice." She remembered the feel of his lips on hers with a pang, but she had to be clear with him. Not that he had to know everything, but she had to tell him something. Give him a reason. Something true.

"Nice?" He looked hurt. "Was?"

She knew if she looked at him, she'd let him lay her down on the twin bed right here in Peach at eight o'clock in the morning. Not gonna happen, and not just because her curtains were wide open.

"Okay, it was better than nice, but help me out here." She struggled to put the right words together.

Daniel stood very still, a puzzled look on his face. "Help you out? Isn't that what I'm doing?"

"I know. With the addition. But what I mean is…" She really didn't want to go into it. "Sit down for a minute."

She moved her laptop from the center of the tiny table in the kitchenette and poured him a cup of coffee. He sat, but didn't touch the coffee.

"I don't want to make a big deal out of this," she said. "I like you. You're nice, you're sweet, you're sexy."

He perked up with those words and took a sip of his coffee.

"But I can't do this. My last boyfriend, we lived together five years, he, uh, well, was older." She took a breath to stop her stammering. It didn't help that Daniel was staring at her over the rim of his coffee mug with those Clark Kent glasses and lake blue eyes. "He had kids. Grown kids. But he promised me we would have a family one day. Together. He strung me along during my most fertile years and dumped me just when my biological clock got a lot more important."

"Whoa." Daniel set his coffee cup down. She didn't know how to interpret that whoa, but after a few beats of silence he started talking again. "Ah, so that means we can't go out. Ticking clock. Time to get serious and settle down. I'm not your man."

He said it so boldly, with no apology, which was better than lying like Marcus, but it still punched a hole in her heart.

She let out a whoosh of held in breath. "Thank you." She was being silly to want more so soon. "I appreciate the honesty."

"Same here. I like you. You don't play games."

She wasn't sure she could say the same about him, but of course he was not going to promise her a lifetime of devotion after a couple of make-out sessions. He didn't know her middle name. He didn't know her birthday or her favorite flavor of ice cream.

He drained his coffee and got up from the chair. "No harm, no foul. Friends it is. Gotta get to work." And he left, carefully closing the door on his way out.

She sat there, stunned with relief and something else she didn't want to think about. After a few minutes, she let it go, immersed herself in work. The most important element to success in her venture was paying customers. How would they reach her? Hear about Blue Heaven? She went into work mode and didn't come up for air until well after dark.

The week passed that way, she in her cottage hammering at the keyboard while Daniel hammered her dream house. She'd seen a few new faces, younger guys Daniel's age. She didn't question him going over her budget and obviously paying them out of his own pocket. His choice. Plus she was too busy adding to her website and riding the first wave of advertising.

She tried not to let it bother her too much that Daniel treated her with distant respect. The sort of politeness reserved for a co-worker with whom he had little in common, but had to work closely with on a project.

That wasn't how she wanted it to be, but she figured he'd eventually warm back up. He'd see it was better to be friends than lovers when work was the main objective, and she could get the whole silly idea of making a family with him out of her system. Even though it hurt to remember, she couldn't forget: he'd heard her proposal, and turned her down flat.

****

On the way to Blue Heaven, Daniel called his editor friend at *Discovery Architecture*. Truth was, Daniel had been pestering this guy for years to do a story on Bryman. He'd humored Daniel without ever committing. Just in time to prove his worth to Eva, the press was finally interested.

"I'm looking at the website now," the journalist said. "It's nice. I like the angle of the two great-grandfathers working together to be flexible during the Depression. Detroit's in a bit of a depression itself, so she's repeating history. And you're helping. Great hook. Bit of a downer though, rough economy brings back Depression era architect."

"But it's a good thing. The whole less-conspicuous consumption idea." Daniel thought fast. He needed to get this spot in *D.A.* for Eva. She would be so happy, she'd forget about that stupid "all work, no play" rule of hers. "We're bringing something back to Michigan that people forgot about. Our lakeshores. Our heritage. Bryman."

"You could do a video, drive around town, film the houses, film the progress at the resort, etcetera. You could read from some of the old letters. Put it on an internet. Create a buzz."

"That's a great idea, thanks."

"And I'll pitch the story to my editor. Not saying she'll buy it, but we have been meaning to do something in the Midwest."

"Let me know what you need."

"Don't worry, I will. Got your number. Mind you, it will be a year probably before this hits an issue, so this friend of yours—she is only a friend, right?"

"For now," Daniel said. They both laughed. Why was it so easy for another guy to understand that sometimes it was okay for friends to come with benefits?

"Well, your *friend* is going to have to build her clientele by word of mouth, at least this season. If I get the go-ahead, it would see print next spring, March or April. I'm not sure. Like I said, I have to get approval from MY boss."

"I'm just glad to finally get some interest."

"I've been interested, I just couldn't find an angle. Now you've handed me one."

They shot the breeze for a bit and then got off the phone. He wouldn't tell Eva about the article until it was a for-sure thing. But he could talk to her about the video. That would be fun. They could do it together. As he pulled off the highway and into Eva's long driveway, he saw the roofers shingling the airplane roof.

****

"Hey, little girl, want to go for a ride in my car?"

If Eva lived to be one hundred fifty years old, she would never understand men. After barely speaking a word to her all week, here was Daniel looking way too happy about working all day right under those thundering hammers.

She thought about saying something to him about being ignored, but then she dropped it. With Lily living at Blue Heaven, she'd gotten good at holding her tongue and picking her battles. Why bring up his week-long sulk when it would just remind him that she'd stopped the physical part of their relationship?

"Come on. The website's done. The roof is on. The ads are out. The brochures are being printed in Port Huron. You're moved back into the bungalow. Let's do something fun. Let's make a video."

"Really?" The idea thrilled her, actually. She'd have done it herself except she couldn't shoot video for crap.

"My buddy at *Discovery Architecture* actually thought of it." The minute the words were out of Daniel's mouth, he clamped his jaws shut like he'd said too much.

Daniel seemed torn about saying anything else, but Eva knew, also from her close contact with Lily, that sometimes, you just wait and the rest of the story will eventually come out. Not that she'd gotten Lily's full story. Yet.

"No promises, but he checked out your website, and he's going to talk to his editor."

"Wow!" Happiness bubbled inside her.

"I know!"

Man, she was glad he had finally gotten over the ignoring her routine!

"So you ready?" he asked.

"We should take the Mustang." Eva checked her pockets for car keys. "We could put the top down."

Perfect. A beautiful day, a gorgeous woman, what more could a guy ask for?

"It's warmer than it's been all spring." The only bad thing about early May was that the days were moving way too fast. She was only half-booked for the summer. Maybe the video would get her reservation numbers up.

Before they could fire up the Mustang, Lily rushed out of her cottage yelling "No no no!" She almost collided with Daniel. When she saw him, she shuddered and turned to Eva, who stood frozen, unsure what was happening.

Bob walked out of Lily's cabin, looking pained. The four stood in an uneasy circle as hammers and saws stilled.

"Back to work," Daniel called out.

The noises of renovation resumed.

Chapter Thirteen

"What happened?"

"What's wrong?" Daniel's and Eva's questions overlapped.

Daniel put a hand on Bob's shoulder; Eva was afraid to touch Lily, who wrapped both arms around herself and muttered, "Nothing."

"Let's walk," Daniel said, his hand, still on Bob's shoulder, guiding Bob toward the empty park next door.

When Lily followed, her head down, not meeting Eva's eyes, Eva, more confused than ever, trooped after everyone toward a bench facing the water at the far end of the park. Nobody sat.

"Sorry, dude," Lily spoke first, to Bob. At least Eva assumed Lily spoke to Bob. She had her head down and wasn't meeting anyone's eyes. Bob looked from Daniel to Lily. Since she couldn't see Lily through the curtain of her hair, Eva tried to read the expression on Bob's face. Confused? Guilty? Sad for sure.

"S'okay," Bob said. "Me too."

Bob and Lily sat down on the bench, carefully keeping space between their bodies, both looking out at the water and not at each other.

Eva met Daniel's eyes over the kids' heads. It had been obvious to everyone in Blue Lake for a while now that Bob had a crush on Lily. Sometimes Lily flirted with Bob, other times she pushed him away. This seemed like something else. Something more serious than two teenagers navigating an attraction.

"Do you want to talk about what happened?" Eva suggested.

"NO!" Bob and Lily said together. Then they looked at each other and smiled.

"Friends?" Bob asked Lily.

"Friends," Lily confirmed.

"You sure you're okay?" Eva asked Lily.

"Stop being a mom. I just get a little crazy sometimes. No big. Sorry to scare you."

"Bob didn't hurt you?" Daniel asked. But he put his hand back on Bob's shoulder when he said it.

Lily shook her head.

"Can we please just drop it?"

"If you're sure—"

Lily looked out over the big water. Bob, next to her, seemed to be holding his breath.

Eva wondered where this left her video ride with Daniel. Should they continue with the day as planned? She glanced at him, the question in her eyes.

Daniel shrugged.

"Well," he said, "if we're done here…"

"You guys want to come with us?" Eva said, before Daniel had a chance to finish his thought.

"I gotta finish the plaster job in the green cottage," Bob said.

"Kiwi," Lily corrected him. "Kiwi Cottage."

"Right."

"I've got laundry to do," Lily admitted. "Where were you guys going, anyway?"

Daniel told them about the video shoot.

"You're going to put the top down, right?" Lily

said. It wasn't a question as much as a plea. "Where's your video camera? You don't want to load a phone video for marketing."

Lily looked at Eva. Eva wondered how Lily knew so much about cameras and marketing.

"Laundry can wait," Eva said.

"You can knock off for the day if you like," Daniel told Bob.

Bob and Lily sprung up and headed toward the break of tall pines that separated Blue Heaven from the park.

"Hope that was okay," Eva said to Daniel after the kids were out of earshot.

"That girl has issues," Daniel said. "But yeah, it's fine."

Later, Eva thought, maybe Lily would tell her what had happened. It probably had to do with Bob innocently taking things to a physical level Lily wasn't comfortable with—that seemed like the obvious thing. Bob was a good kid, but he was a teenaged boy. At least whatever happened seemed to have stopped before they'd gone too far.

The top on her Mustang was already down when they got to the car. Lily and Bob sat in the back seat.

"This is so cool!" Lily said, as if nothing had happened. "I *love* convertibles! Daniel, can I see your camera?"

****

Daniel felt happy and sad. Relieved that the neurotic chick had simmered down and was not, according to Bob, on any drugs. "She doesn't even smoke pot," Bob had said when Daniel asked. So that part was all good. The not so good part was that since they had the kids along, there was no way he was going to get a chance to change Eva's mind about the moratorium on kissing. He'd been thinking about it all week, and he had a sort of plan that would get her at least into his arms. If she said yes. Big if. But he had to try.

For now, he pointed to the just-opened Very Blue ice cream stand. It was like the ice cream people had a direct line to the weather, because every spring, on the warmest day of May, they miraculously opened, giving locals a chance to enjoy their downtown before the tourists took over.

The four of them sat at a picnic table, licking their cones, while Daniel plotted ways to get more of Eva's attention. She was pretty much ignoring him and focusing on Lily, asking her what she thought were subtle questions about where she was from and why she'd left home in the first place.

Lily might be a bit high maintenance for Daniel's tastes, but he had to hand it to the girl—she could handle Eva better than he ever had.

"All the towns up here are alike," Lily said, avoiding the question. "What I want to know is how it feels to work in a big city like Detroit."

"Honey, I worked in Bloomfield Hills."

"How far is that from Detroit? Did you ever go to Red Wings games? You know, live?"

Daniel stopped listening. It wasn't that he didn't care about Eva's life before Blue Lake. More that he wanted it to be him asking the questions.

When he finished his cone, he laid out his plan.

"Eva, if you wouldn't mind, I'll drive, and Bob can shoot the video of the town."

"Can I? Please?" Lily asked. "I took a videography class last year," she said. "It was cool."

"Sure," Bob said.

Eva clutched her car keys with one hand, her half eaten cone with the other. She didn't seem ready to hand him over her keys.

"If I drive, then we don't have all the directions, *Turn here, go here, stop there* on the video. I can give you and the internet the Bryman tour. It will flow better. Trust me."

When Eva still didn't give him her keys, even after he'd handed his top-of-the-line video camera over to Lily, he started to get irritated. He had to tamp down his annoyance. Women! What exactly was the problem?

"I haven't had a traffic ticket. Ever." He tried to smile sweetly, hiding his disappointment with how the day was turning out. Earlier, he'd had such high hopes for this day. But it was fine. He could initiate Mission: Fast Eddie later.

Finally, she gave him the keys.

Score one for me, Daniel thought.

"Do you need to sit up front, Lily?" Eva asked.

And it's a tie. Again.

"No. It's actually better back here—" Lily was already back in the car, pointing the camera here and there, checking the shots. "No windshield or mirrors to get in the way."

Eva sat in the front seat, next to him.

Nice save.

Now if they could just lose the junior adults. Daniel didn't mean that. He loved Bob. The kids had spring fever, obviously needed a diversion. He'd work on getting closer to Eva another day. Or maybe tonight.

Daniel's mood improved as he took Eva through town, showing off all the Bryman homes he'd helped restore. He wanted to take her inside every single place, show her what he could do with cracked plaster and worn wood.

"I'd love you to see the built-ins Bryman crafted himself," Daniel said. He was thinking maybe some of the owners would be willing to open their homes to a tour at some point.

"How do you know which parts of the house he did himself?"

"He carved his initials, VB, very tiny on the back or the bottom of the wood."

"Like a silver hallmark."

Daniel didn't know from silver, but he nodded, just happy to be with her.

"Show them the museum, bro," Bob said. "And then let's go grab some Mexican. I think Sanchez's is open."

Daniel took a left. He pulled into the museum's driveway and put Eva's car in park. He turned off the ignition.

"Maybe the ladies don't like Mexican food," he said.

"I love it," Lily said, piling out of the car, the camera firmly in her grip. "Are we going inside this one?"

****

After they'd toured the museum and found seats on the sidewalk tables of Sanchez's, Eva ordered a margarita. Mr. and Mrs. Sanchez both knew Daniel and Bob and treated them like family, making a fuss over them, wiping off the already spotless plastic seating, bringing them extra tortilla chips.

"They're really Mexican, then?" Lily said. "I'm going to get authentic enchiladas instead of the Taco Bell version?"

"Yep. Their parents were migrant workers who settled in the area, so we lucked out and have a true taste of Mexico in Michigan."

"Lucked out?" Bob said. "Did you forget that you loaned them the money to open this place?"

Daniel didn't say anything, just studied the menu.

"Don't you mean the bank loaned them the money?" Eva crunched one of the fresh chips dipped in salsa after she asked the question.

"Nope. Daniel always loans people money when the bank won't. Out of his own pocket. With no interest."

That was the same thing he'd offered her, Eva realized.

"Only when I think they deserve a chance, like the Sanchez family."

Now their utter devotion to Daniel made more sense. As Eva tried the guacamole, she had to admit that Daniel had been right about the food. She licked the salt on the rim of her cocktail and sipped the icy drink. Divine.

"So, what did you think of the museum?" Daniel asked her.

She thought the barter was fair. The place was in even worse shape than Blue Heaven had been when she'd taken occupancy. But it would be fun, too. The best part is that she had an unlimited budget, free reign to do what she wanted, and six months instead of two to complete her winter project.

"It'll be a blast," she said, editing her thoughts down to their essence.

"We need to get you a webcam laptop so I can see the progress in real time."

"Okay, Big Brother," Eva said, not comfortable with the idea that Daniel would be so far away, but teasing him in order to avoid thinking about why she wanted him here, with her.

Lily chatted to Bob about her video class; it was as if the earlier upset this afternoon had never happened. Bob was as smitten as ever, obvious because he hung on Lily's every word.

"You should do something with that," Eva told Lily.

"Like what?"

"I don't know. What do people who love video do? Go to film school? Try to meet Michael Moore?"

"You could set up a Vlog," Bob said.

Eva had no idea what that even was. Sounded like something from Star Trek.

Lily looked pensive.

"I haven't really thought about it," she finally said, right before their dinners arrived, fragrant and steaming.

The last of the sun lowered in the sky, the last of the meals had been scraped from the plates, when Bob said "Aunt Jane!" the pleasure in his voice evident on his face.

Chapter Fourteen

As it had been for most of the day, downtown was alive with locals. Eva looked to where Bob was directing his beams of happiness and easily picked out Jane, just turning the key on a building next door to Sanchez's. Jane looked up, saw them, and smiled. She threw her keys into her purse and came over to where they sat.

Their waiter quickly found another chair while Daniel ordered Spanish coffees for himself and Eva and Mexican hot chocolate for the kids. Daniel was sweet and thoughtful. As the sun went down, the day had cooled a bit, and he didn't want her to catch a chill. He eyed Jane, who kissed Bob, then directed the waiter to place the extra chair between Daniel and Eva.

"I'll have a Chardonnay," Jane said. "Stocked my brand yet?"

The waiter nodded and went to fill their drink order.

"You might as well just bring the bottle," Jane called after him.

Eva worried about Jane's liver, but admired how she handled her liquor. She herself was glad Daniel was driving her car. Just the one potent margarita had given her a glow that was probably over the legal limit, and she was sure the Spanish coffee would do nothing to sober her up. "What have you people been up to, besides eating everything in Sanchez's kitchen?" Jane sipped the wine the waiter had rushed over to her.

As Bob recapped the day, Eva realized the building Jane had just locked up was her office. She was so glad she didn't have to be cooped up all day anymore at the agency, but could make her own schedule. Of course, Jane did that too. She showed houses and made deals. Not that there were many real estate deals to be made in Michigan right now.

"I hope you're not slowing down on your renovations," Jane said to Eva.

"Heck no," Bob answered for her. "We've got every skilled laborer in town on one job or the other."

This was news to Eva, as no workers had been present at the museum when they'd toured it, although she was relieved that her crew was not being overworked.

"I'm sure their families appreciate the paychecks," Jane said, turning toward Daniel as she spoke.

Eva tried, but she couldn't feel any special vibe between Daniel and Jane. Nothing more than old friendship. Jane didn't spend any extra time talking to Daniel, but asked Lily about film, Bob about college, and Eva about the progress on the cottages.

Eva asked Jane about her job and this was the only time Jane's easy smile faltered. She poured another glass of wine and said "Things are slow." Then she drank a hefty swallow and stared into her glass.

Obviously the wrong topic, Eva thought.

But then Daniel told a funny story about the previous owners of the museum and how they'd had all these bizarre requirements for selling, and how Jane had humored their every whim, including the one that said the new owner had to leave a certain rocking chair in the room at the top of the stairs for the ghost.

Eva remembered seeing the rocking chair and finding it charming but empty of any ghost. She laughed with everyone else, including Jane. Was Jane glowing a little more than usual? Was it from the wine or Daniel's bragging about her patience and expertise? Eva couldn't tell, but since Jane's body language didn't betray any special interest in Daniel, not even in the flutter of a lash, she relaxed. They were just old pals, they enjoyed each other's company, and that was it. Not that it mattered. Not that she cared.

As they drove home, the kids opting to hang out downtown and then walk back to Blue Heaven later, Eva asked Daniel about Jane. She was pretty sure there was nothing but friendship, but still wanted to get Daniel's side of the story. Jane's depiction of their affair and Daniel's morals were a little darker than Eva's read. She was simply curious, she told herself. Nothing personal.

"We were kids when we dated," Daniel said.

"She said she was like a mom to Bob."

"Her mother was like a mom to Bob. Along with my grandmother and half the town's female population. Jane cared about Jane. Then and now and always."

She mulled that over. Daniel and Jane seemed perfectly comfortable with each other, friendly even, and yet, each had slightly negative things to say about the other. At least to her. She hoped he wasn't thinking she was jealous, or that she cared. Maybe she did, a little, even though she didn't want to.

Back at Blue Heaven, Daniel decided to get some shots of the beach. The full moon was so bright there was no need for a flashlight as they walked down the steps Daniel had built. Eva was grateful for the handrail, and for the sweater she'd grabbed out of the bungalow before going down to the water with Daniel.

When they got to the shore, Lily was there, her arms folded, staring out at the moon's reflection in the lake.

Daniel shot her in profile, her features barely discernible by the light of the moon.

"The romantic getaway of a lifetime," he said for the benefit of the camera.

Lily turned around and glared.

"Did I say you could film me?"

"Turn it off, Daniel," Eva said.

"No, that's fine, I can edit her out. Although I don't remember you asking any of us for permission to film today, Lily."

"Hey, don't, Daniel," Eva said as Lily stomped off.

"I was kidding," he replied. "That girl is so touchy." After filming the moon and the water for a few more minutes, he turned off the camera and set it on the steps.

"Want to go for a walk?" Daniel asked.

"No," Eva said. A romantic moonlit walk sounded lovely. But she had better not. It was bad enough they'd spent the day together.

"I should really go see if Lily wants to tell me what happened today."

"Bob already told me."

"When?"

"While Bob and I checked the museum roof repairs."

Right. She'd forgotten.

"Well? What happened?"

"They were kissing and things got a little intense and he took her obvious pleasure in what was happening as permission to move to the next level. She freaked."

"I thought it might be something like that."

"I also gave Bob strict instructions to keep his hands, and his mouth, to himself."

"Really?" Eva wondered how you could tell an eighteen year old to do that, and if there was a chance in hell they'd listen.

"I told her that girl is bad news and that he should steer clear."

Eva resented Daniel's assessment.

"Maybe she's a virgin. Maybe she'd never been felt up before. Maybe she's got Catholic guilt or something. I know I did when I was her age. That doesn't make her *bad news.*"

Eva wasn't sure why she was becoming so upset with the Daniel/Bob version of events. It was just that men were so, what was the word, so obvious in their single-minded quest for sex?

Daniel was quiet for a minute after Eva's outburst.

"Okay, now I suppose you think I have *issues* too?"

He went over and picked up his camera. "We all have issues. I didn't mean to criticize Lily. It's just...she's more than a handful. I don't want Bob to have to deal with all her drama. If that sounds cold, well, it's also realistic. Bob's a simple guy. He wouldn't hurt her. I don't want him to be hurt, because, let's face it, he's the one who's interested. She's not. So, he should just back off. That's all I was saying."

He started up the steps. Eva followed.

"Okay, I see your point," she said. "You're trying to protect him."

"I dated Jane. I know about girls with issues. They are so not worth the trouble they bring."

Eva didn't want to get angry at Daniel. She saw that he cared about his brother. But she cared about Lily. And Jane. Daniel, in her opinion, was giving both of them a raw deal.

She sighed. This was not the time to talk to Daniel about Lily. He likely didn't even mean the word the way it sounded, as if Lily's intrinsic worth was wrapped up in her inability to be sexual with Bob. She didn't want to get into the Jane thing. Daniel and Jane obviously had different perceptions of their earlier relationship, but the important thing was that they'd let it go, they'd moved on, they were friends. Eva admired that.

"You're probably right," she finally said. "Bob should keep his distance. And I should talk to Lily to see if I can figure out a way to help her—if there's more wrong than the simple fact that she's just not that into Bob."

"Ouch," Daniel said.

Eva walked toward the lakefront door, leaving Daniel to walk to his car alone.

Inside, Lily sat watching television. Eva tried to talk to her.

"You okay?"

"Sure. Just bored. There's nothing on television."

Okay, so Lily was a bit of a brat. After a day of driving around, eating ice cream, and enjoying dinner downtown, she was still bored. Teenagers were tough.

Eva didn't know how Daniel had done it with Bob, and at such a young age.

Lily's feet were bare, as they had been down at the beach. Eva didn't know how she could walk on the rocky shoreline without shoes, but Lily said when you grew up on the lake, you got used to it. She wondered if Lily had been down at the lake looking for her own coastal town.

"So whereabouts on the lake are you from?"

"Not too far from here," Lily said.

"Really? What town?"

"Why does that matter?" Lily shut down again.

"I guess it doesn't," Eva said. But she knew something was really bothering Lily. She wished she knew what it was.

"Let's celebrate," Eva said. It was an impulse, but her instincts were all she had when it came to Lily.

Lily looked up from a rerun of an old sitcom.

"Why?"

"Well, maybe celebrate is not the exact word. Just have a free day."

"Wasn't that what today was supposed to be?"

"Nope. We were working. And you deserve a bonus for doing all that filming."

Eva had gotten the idea from looking at Lily's bare feet.

"We should have a spa day. Get our hair cut, mani-pedi, whatever."

"You mean it?"

"Yeah. We can get the laundry going tonight and finish it in the morning, and then take the afternoon off for pampering."

Lily held up her hand. Her pretty manicure had

been destroyed by all the work she'd done. Her fingernails had tones of peach, blue, and yellow.

"I could use a facial," Lily said.

"Let me call some salons in Port Huron and see if I can book us appointments."

"When do you think Daniel will have the video posted?"

"He's going to work on it tonight. Maybe later."

"I can't wait to see it!"

Eva went to load a heap of towels, while Lily gathered up shopping bags of sheets and toted them into the laundry room behind Eva.

"Why do we have to wash these when we bought them new from the store?" Lily pulled the linens out of their packaging, snipping tags as she went along.

Eva hoped the video would bring in more business. So far, July and part of August were booked, but she needed customers in June if she didn't want to use all her emergency funds paying her bank loan.

Chapter Fifteen

Eva's phone rang. She checked caller ID. Daniel.

"Hi." She walked toward the office and her laptop. Maybe he had the video up already.

But no, he told her, he'd given the hours of footage to a friend from high school who was going to whittle it down to a couple of minutes.

"It seems a shame to waste it all," Eva commented.

"And it's really good. Lily has a gift for shooting."

"I'll tell her you said that." Eva was just relieved that Daniel had warmed back up to the girl.

"I was thinking…" Daniel said hesitating.

"What?"

"Do you think maybe we could make a movie of the town, you know, for the museum? Or maybe I could get a website built?"

"Of course." Eva wished she'd thought of it first. "I've been so busy with my own marketing, but I'll have time this summer to get something online for the museum. And it should have a name. Bryman House?"

"I like it," Daniel said, his voice warm.

"Good." Eva liked collaborating with Daniel this way. If only it was always this easy.

"So I'll see you tomorrow," he said.

"Maybe for a bit," she replied. "I've made some appointments for Lily and myself in Port Huron. Girl stuff."

"Oh? Well, after you girls get your hair done, or whatever it is you're up to, why don't you meet Bob and me for dinner and a movie?" Daniel said.

Eva had learned that going to Port Huron in Blue Lake was a major event. And she would have stayed in Blue Lake, but they didn't have a day spa. Or a movie theater.

"That might be fun." Lily had mentioned something about a vampire movie.

"Let's do it for the kids," he said.

"Well, sure, okay. For the kids," she said.

Eva hung up, her spirits buoyed. She immediately began justifying her happiness. This wasn't a date. It was for the kids. And it would be a shame to waste a professional blow dry. Her hair, naturally curly, got absolutely frizzy living so near the water.

She went to find Lily, to ask about the movie project. Actually, since he was going to be using her work publicly, Eva would talk to Daniel about paying Lily for her filming.

Lily stood at the washer, wearing a baggy pair of sweatpants that Eva was sure must belong to Bob, loading several pair of jeans into the machine.

Eva hadn't realized she'd been on the phone with Daniel through an entire cycle of laundry. But the neat stack of towels on the folding table told the story. And there was another story here in this room, too.

"Could you loan me, like, a robe or some pajamas?"

Eva felt saddened that she hadn't paid much attention to Lily's lack of wardrobe before. She'd given the girl the hoodie she'd appropriated on her first day at Blue Heaven, plus a few old shirts for layering, but that had been the extent of her generosity. Lily had probably been sleeping in T-shirts. And after today's episode with Bob, she'd be feeling vulnerable.

"Of course. Why don't you go take a bath? It's been a long day."

She'd find Lily some pajamas, make her another hot chocolate, and tell her the good news about the footage she'd shot today. And the movie tomorrow would be the cherry on top.

Lily left the room, holding the sweatpants up so they didn't fall to her feet.

Eva went into her room and found some yoga pants, a terry cloth robe that was way too long for her, and a couple pair of camisole and brushed cotton pajamas, one with shorts and one with long bottoms. Lord knew she had more than enough to spare Lily a few things.

The bathroom door was closed. She could hear the water running in the tub. She put the stack of clothes on the hallway table, knocked on the door. "Use the lavender bubble bath," she said. "It's super relaxing. And I've got your robe and things out here on the hall table.

"Thanks," Lily called.

Eva again wondered whose child she was and if her folks were worried that she'd left. Eighteen or twenty-eight, Lily would always be somebody's child. Eva remembered the fluffy bunny slippers her mom had brought her for Easter. She'd been busy getting ready to move to Florida, but had taken the time to fill a basket for her only child, as she did every year. The slippers had been cute but too small. They were somewhere in the back of her closet. Maybe they'd fit Lily.

After she put the slippers next to the pile of clothes, she went to switch the jeans from washer to dryer and fold the new cottage linens. One less job for Lily to do.

Waiting for Lily, she checked reservations on the website again. A few more had trickled in, but by now she should really be fully booked. Then Lily walked in, freshly scrubbed and wearing the bunny slippers and robe.

"Video up yet?"

Eva closed the computer and shook her head. "But Daniel loved your footage." She walked with Lily into the kitchen and got out the milk for hot chocolate, happy when she noticed the can of fake whipped cream on the shelf. Bob liked to point the can at his mouth and squirt, so Eva never knew if there would be any left. She'd gotten into the habit of buying a can a week.

Lily sat at the tiny kitchen table, the moon shining in through the little window, waiting for her hot chocolate.

"This won't be as good at the one you had at Sanchez's," Eva warned, scooping the powdered cocoa into the pan with the milk.

"We were kissing," Lily said.

Eva already knew that, but she didn't say so. Lily would hate it if she knew they'd been talking about her.

"And he kinda put his hands…well, I panicked."

"That's okay. You're entitled to feel your feelings any time a boy does anything to make you feel uncomfortable."

Eva poured the hot drink into two mugs and sat down across from Lily.

"Everything okay now?"

Lily nodded, sipping her chocolate.

"Good," Eva said, and then told Lily about dinner and the movie.

Lily put her mug down. "It's weird," she said.

Eva waited. This was the longest conversation about something personal she and Lily had ever had.

"I'm, you know, attracted to him. But it's just no good."

Eva knew exactly what Lily meant. She was not going to press Lily on the details. If Lily wanted to talk, she knew Eva was there to listen.

"Bob understands," Eva said. "He saw how upset you were. He won't kiss you again."

"This is so hard," Lily said.

"I know, honey."

"Thanks for the pajamas."

"If we have time tomorrow, we'll go shopping. You probably need a few things."

"I could use some undies," Lily said, then giggled. Then she yawned.

"It's been a long day. I'll fold the jeans for you."

Still, Lily sat at the table.

"Do you want to sleep in here tonight?" Eva said.

"I wouldn't mind," Lily admitted. "But it might hurt Bob's feelings."

"Well, if he noticed, we could say you fell asleep watching television."

Eva usually kicked the kids out at 11 p.m.

"I'll get some sheets and make up the sofa. You'll be the first one to use the pull-out."

"Okay," Lily said.

When Eva brought sheets and blankets into the living room, Lily had lowered all the bamboo shades. Eva went over and locked the door. Lily's spine visibly sagged. Relief, Eva sensed. She wasn't sure what was going on, but for whatever reason, Lily had not felt safe tonight, even though she had seemed perfectly at ease with Bob all day. And worried about what he'd think tonight.

"I'm going to lock the office door tonight, too," Eva usually left it open for Lily or Bob. Mostly Lily, who liked her baths and Eva's beauty products. "Just in case we want to sleep in. We don't need any of the crew busting in on us."

They made up the sofa bed together.

"You know, we could get your room in here ready, if you want. It might be easier to get the cottage sorted for guests if you had another place to sleep."

"Okay," Lily said, clicking on the remote, but turning the volume low and programming it to turn off in thirty minutes.

" 'Night," Lily said, her eyes half shut.

Eva wasn't tired at all. She decided to start fooling around with a website for Bryman House. It felt good to begin to pay Daniel back for all the free work he was doing here at Blue Heaven.

Chapter Sixteen

The next morning, she showed Daniel the temporary website for his museum.

"This is what we see, but if anyone Googles 'Bryman House' they'll see this." Eva clicked over to the "Under Construction" icon she'd posted and then back to the temporary site that needed to be filled with info and photos and the video.

"Excellent," Daniel said.

Eva agreed. She hadn't slept much last night, and she'd heard Lily tossing and turning, too. But they'd made it through, and later, they'd relax at the spa.

Lily came into the office, having already erased any hint of having slept in the bungalow. The living room was back to normal and she was dressed in fresh jeans and the concert T-shirt Eva gave her the night before. It was old, from back when the band was still mostly a local Detroit act, but not beat up. Eva wasn't really a concert T-shirt sort of person, although she always bought them when she attended shows. She had a drawerful that never got any use. Maybe Lily would like them.

"Hey," Lily said to Daniel.

"You two see the video yet?"

They hadn't. Eva had been so into building Daniel's website, she hadn't thought once about checking her reservations or to see if the video was up.

She'd have to put a link on her site before they left for the spa.

Daniel typed into the keyboard and the video came up. They watched how his friend had edited their day yesterday to make a fast, fun, clip. They ran the clip a couple more times.

"I didn't know you filmed me," she said, looking at Lily.

"I didn't," Lily said.

Eva checked again. Daniel had still been filming then, because she'd been driving, her hair blowing in the wind, the sunlight catching her smile. In voiceover, Daniel said, "Meet Eva Delacroix, owner of Blue Heaven, a special vacation spot in Blue Lake, Michigan."

"I look at you a lot when you don't know I'm looking," he said.

Her heart skidded.

"Lily, your footage is awesome," Eva said, embarrassed. She tried to focus as the video panned the town, the pretty painted cottages, and the beach, with quick cuts to Frank and Sam on the roof of the bungalow.

Daniel's film-buff friend ended the clip with the shot of the moon on the water and Daniel saying "Come see the moonlight on the sunrise side of the state. Visit Blue Heaven on beautiful Lake Huron this summer."

Her website address flashed on the screen. She clicked on the link and her site appeared. She clicked on reservations and couldn't believe it.

"You did it. I'm fully booked for the season."

"Well, my friend put it together. He loved your footage, Lily. Said you've got raw talent."

Lily smiled and twirled away. She'd been cleaning out the spare room she'd chosen, squeezing bags and boxes and lamps all into one room to make way for a bed and dresser that Eva would still have to find. She'd ordered a mattress last night online.

Lily bounced back into the room.

"I can pick out what color I want to paint my room, right?"

Daniel looked at Eva, shrugged, and walked up the staircase he'd managed to salvage from the ruin of Frank and Sam's work.

"Sure, honey," Eva said. She looked at the time on her computer. "We need to leave here in a half hour or so."

"No problem," Lily said.

Eva clicked into her email account, but Lily still hovered nearby.

"What is it, hon?"

Eva's email box was jammed and the newsfeed had a headline about 500 Detroit advertising people out of jobs. She clicked it open, then turned to listen to Lily, who was uncharacteristically silent.

"I know I'm being a pain and all, but could I keep the cottage and the bedroom for now?"

"Well, of course. And you're not a pain."

"But can I sleep in the living room sometimes until my bedroom in here is done?"

Eva wondered if she should try to dig deeper into Lily's unease. Surely Bob could not be the cause of this.

"It's not Bob. Honest. I just," Lily sighed, "can't talk about it."

"You can sleep wherever you feel comfortable,"

Eva said. "At least until we get your bedroom all set."

"So I can keep my stuff in the cottage, but, like, crash in here?"

"Yep."

"Cool."

Lily started to head out into the yard, but then pivoted back in. "But don't tell Bob. He'll feel bad. And he shouldn't."

"I won't tell Bob."

"Or Daniel."

"Or Daniel."

"You better get off that computer or we're going to be late for our appointments," Lily said.

Eva quickly read the report that her former agency had just closed their offices in Detroit. God, how much worse could it get? She spent a couple minutes answering a few emails from her closest friends still at the agency.

Even Marcus had lost his job.

Everyone had seen it coming, so they weren't as upset as Eva had been when she'd gotten laid off. They wanted to know about her, how she was doing, if her project was on schedule, when they could visit. She knew the truth, even if they didn't. They'd be too busy looking for work to spend time with her this summer. Still, she extended the invitation. She planned to have a guest room ready to go when she opened in June.

"Come on, Eva," Lily said.

"I'm leaving," Eva called up to Daniel after she'd logged off her computer.

"See you at dinner," he said.

****

Eva and Lily spent the day together, but they never

got a chance to talk. The salon ladies made a fuss over them, or blow-dryers were running, or Lily was getting her facial while Eva had a massage.

Still, after their mani-pedis were dry, they had an hour before they were supposed to meet the guys for dinner.

"Time to shop," Eva said. "My treat."

Lily looked adorable, fresh, and ready to rock the mall.

Maybe it wasn't about getting Lily to open up about whatever made her leave home with little more than the clothes on her back. Maybe it was simply about taking care of her in the here and now. Somehow this grouchy girl, who lit up like Christmas at the thought of some shopping, had gotten under Eva's skin.

Eva thought for a minute about her budget, but pushed away any nervousness about spending even more money than she'd dropped at the salon. This day was doing wonders for Lily. It was worth every penny.

Lily chose jeans, little half boots, and a gauzy tunic. Eva found a white dress with big red poppies all over it that matched her nail polish. When she would have stuck with her plain black ballet flats, Lily had insisted she buy the adorable pair of red kitten heels.

"If you don't buy footwear, neither will I, and you know I only have one pair of sneakers. Which are like some weird art shoes now with all the paint splatters."

It was true, so Eva bought the shoes. And some new sneakers for Lily, budget be damned.

****

Daniel watched Eva approach the table, vaguely aware of Lily at her side. Eva was more radiant than he'd ever seen her, and not just because she'd had something nice done to her hair that made it extra shiny and swingy. Maybe it was the dress, the way it scooped low, skimming the tops of her breasts. With extreme effort, Daniel banished thoughts of how he'd had her in his bed, he'd briefly held those breasts. And somehow he'd messed up and that's all he was ever going to get of her unless he could woo her into intimacy with Mission: Fast Eddie.

"May I bring you something to drink?"

The waitress appeared the moment Lily and Eva sat. Lily and Bob ordered Cokes, and Daniel bent closer than was probably necessary to Eva, asking if she'd like to choose a bottle of wine. She smelled like flowers and something else deeper and more mysterious.

Eva flipped open the menu and said, "You know what I've been craving all day?"

He only wished it were him.

"A strawberry milk shake."

"We can do that," said the waitress.

Daniel ordered coffee. He had a feeling he'd need it during the movie. He had zero interest in the whole vampire craze.

He looked at Eva next to him, ran his eyes over her body as discreetly as possible. He didn't think he'd ever seen her legs before. When she sat, a lot of them showed. They were lovely. Her throat clearing signaled that she noticed him staring.

"Great shoes," he said, although if she asked what color they were, he'd be unmasked as a liar. But was it his fault that he was interested in this new Eva, the Eva underneath the jeans and work shirts?

"Thanks," she said, about the shoes.

"You look very pretty tonight," he said.

She blushed.

He didn't compliment her enough. He should do that more often. But surely she knew how lovely she was? How her face made his heart ache because, for whatever silly reasons, she wouldn't let him kiss her anymore?

"Get a room," Lily said.

Bob snickered.

Eva rolled her eyes at the kids.

"Don't mind them. They don't get out much."

To Daniel, the situation was surreal. This wasn't a date. Not really. More of a family outing, although they made a weird family.

"Eva," Bob said, grabbing a dinner roll as soon as the basket hit the table, "how do you want me to adjust the payroll for Logan and Tom?"

"Don't," Daniel said. Damn it. He'd meant to speak to Bob about the skilled carpenters he'd hired on his own dime.

"Those are the new guys I saw working on the addition last week?"

Bob nodded.

"Yeah," Daniel said. He knew she could be touchy about her project. "Don't worry about paying them. They owe me a favor."

He could see the wheels turning in Eva's mind.

"Well," Bob went on, oblivious to the minefield he'd stepped into, "we should only pay Sam half days. That's all he's been good for."

"Does he have a family to support?" Eva asked.

"Wife, grown kids. A couple grandkids, I think."

"Well, then just continue to pay him the daily rate."

"If you're sure."

She tried to be tough, but Daniel knew that deep inside she was a softie. She sucked on her milkshake, which was possibly the sexiest thing he'd ever seen, while Daniel tried to gauge her reaction to Logan and Tom, but he was totally distracted by her cherry-lipsticked mouth covering the bright pink straw.

At the show, they had to split up. Apparently many teenage girls, plus their mothers and boyfriends, liked vampires. Lily and Bob sat two rows in front of them. While the previews aired, Daniel said, "I wish you'd let me pay for dinner. I know how much Bob eats. Your grocery bill has to be huge."

"Well, you're one up on me then," she whispered, "because I have no clue how much skilled carpenters get paid these days, but I'm betting it's more than a hundred bucks a day."

Yep. She was still pissed. He'd only been trying to help get her back into her house sooner. Also he wanted the best workmanship possible, and that just was not possible with the town drunk and a roofer.

"You'll pay me back this winter. Six months of trudging through the cold and snow every day just about equals what the trades pay."

"Sounds like fun."

Fun. Huh. She hadn't lived through a Blue Lake winter yet.

Chapter Seventeen

Daniel hadn't paid much attention to the movie. He'd been too busy trying to figure out exactly when he could get Eva's place done and how much time that left him until September and whether Eva would agree to at least come to Fast Eddie's and meet his friends, because she needed friends, not just Jane, and then he could ask her to dance. He'd make sure it was a slow one and then he could hold her body very close to his.

"The kids behaved well tonight." Daniel got out of the car, stood with Eva as Lily and Bob retreated to their cottages. It was now or never. Do or die. If she said no…he wouldn't think about that.

"Lily's been dying to see that movie."

"What? Er, what about you?"

"I like *True Blood* better." He had no idea what she was talking about so he skipped over that.

"You—"

"You—"

They both said the word at the same time. "You first," Daniel said.

"You were a good sport tonight," she said. The night temperature had cooled and she rubbed her pretty arms with her newly polished fingernails. She turned and headed for her own door.

"It's not about that," he said, following her. He couldn't lose this opportunity. He had to nail the Fast

Eddie plan tonight. "It's what you do when you're a parent. You put them first."

Eva opened the door to the office, the next room on his list to tackle. The wood registration counter was like a siren calling him. "I know what you mean," she said, oblivious that he'd followed her into the house. "I felt a little like that today. I'd never have taken a day off work to blow time and money at a salon if I hadn't wanted to cheer up Lily."

She stopped in the office, clearly realizing now that he had come in behind her.

"Staining and varnishing the old counter and the staircase are my next priority," he said, thinking fast. "I wanted to run something by you."

"About the office?"

She didn't move out of the neutral territory of the office and into her quarters, even though Mama was crying on the other side of the pocket door.

"No, not work. Play. You need to get to know the people our age in this town. We have a thing about going up to Fast Eddie's Friday nights. No dates or anything. Just whoever is available shows up."

"Jane?"

"No. Jane is a loner. But you're not. I can tell. I want you to meet my friends."

"Are you setting me up? Is there going to be some single guy who has my resume?"

If only she knew how far from the truth that was. He was the guy who knew her resume. And he was the guy setting her up. For himself.

"Promise. Nobody knows anything about you, but they're all curious. Say you'll come."

She stood there looking up at the ceiling like it had

an answer. She twisted her lips to one side of her face. After a few disheartening beats, she said yes.

"Yes! This coming Friday. I can pick you up."

"I'll meet you there."

"Nineish."

"Okayish."

Instead of pressing his luck, he went home, mission—for now—accomplished.

Chapter Eighteen

The week flew by as every aspect of the renovation and grand opening got checked off the list. Eva could afford to take a night off and meet Daniel and his friends at Fast Eddie's. She studied her closet for the right jeans and wished Jane was going to be there. She selected her dressier dark jeans. They made her look taller and were the proper length for dancing shoes. She slipped on her favorite ankle boots with wedge heels that were surprisingly comfortable.

When, five minutes later, she pulled into the parking lot, the place was jammed.

Daniel shot up from a table full of people and pitchers of beer the minute she walked in the door. He hustled over to her side, gave her a kiss on the cheek, and brought her to the table. Her cheek still tingled. Oh man. She hoped this was not a mistake.

"Hey everybody, this is Eva." Daniel's voice raised above the band. She stood for a minute feeling awkward as Daniel rattled off names. Nobody offered to shake her hand, but every one of them smiled. She recognized a few guys from the work crew. She smiled at the sea of faces and waved as she sat down next to Daniel at two open seats near the end of a long table.

The bar was loud, but the music was good. The only names she remembered were Luke, who she had contracted for lawn and snow services, and Meg, the woman on the other side of her. Luke offered Eva a beer from a communal pitcher, but eying Meg's glass of sparkling water, which had been served in a wine glass, Eva wondered if they still carried that great brand Jane had loved so much.

A waitress in Daisy Dukes came up and rubbed her hip on Daniel's shoulder. Eva was sure the touch was deliberate even though Daniel ignored it.

"Don't worry about her," Meg said. "Flirts with everyone. You'll see." Eva didn't know how to tell Meg that she was not Daniel's date, just a friend. She didn't feel like just a friend. She felt like pushing Ms. Daisy Dukes onto the floor.

The waitress pretended to finally notice Eva. "What can I get for you, darlin'?" She batted her lashes like a silent movie queen. Meg elbowed Eva and snickered.

"Do you still have Jane Augustine's wine brand? She called it KJ?"

The waitress nodded. "It's on special," she said.

"That's what I'll have."

"Another for me, too, Kitty." Meg held up her almost empty glass, finished it off, and handed the empty to the waitress.

"Is Kitty really her name?" Eva asked Meg.

"Yep. It's on her birth certificate."

The band started playing an old Bob Seger song, "Turn the Page." Everyone in Michigan loved Bob Seger. He was a hometown boy made good who never left. But this was really amazing. Everyone at the table except Daniel, Luke, and Eva got up and walked over to the dance floor.

"You two go ahead," Luke said.

"No way." Eva and Daniel said it together and then laughed. When he'd recommended Luke's services for her resort, Daniel had told Eva Luke had gone through a horrible breakup. No need to make him feel worse by leaving him alone while everyone else danced.

"So is everyone married except the three of us?" Eva asked.

Luke laughed. "Only most of them."

Kitty came by with her wine. "There you go, sweetheart." Huge smile, hand on hip, she waited for Eva to take a sip and nod that the wine was excellent. Then she turned and flirted outrageously with Luke. He mostly ignored her, and she left when someone across the room hollered her name.

By the time Daniel and Luke filled her in on the dating couples, the married pairs, and the singles, the song was over and everyone came back to the table.

The band started up a loud Red Hot Chili Pepper number and Meg sat down, gulping her water. "I'm so thirsty!"

"What's his story?" Eva asked, as Luke got up and headed for the men's room.

"We're all trying to help him get over his busted heart. It ain't easy."

Eva nodded.

"They lived together. It was totally serious. On his part, at least. So I know you own Blue Heaven. And you're dating Daniel now?"

Eva tried to wipe the scowl off her face before Meg noticed. "No, just friends."

"I don't think he thinks so."

"Oh, he knows. He's just pretending he doesn't."

They sipped their drinks and friended each other on

Facebook as the song wound down and another started up. Meg took their picture and tagged Eva. Eva didn't recognize this song. When had she stopped listening to new music?

Some people got up to dance again as the band switched singers. Kitty set down her tray and took a mic, starting a version of "Girls Just Wanna Have Fun" that wasn't awful. Her perky dance moves and expressive face were great and her voice was in tune most of the time.

Eva noticed only women on the dance floor. Figures. No guy was going to dance to that song.

"Come on." Meg took Eva's hand and pulled her onto the dance floor. "It's a Blue Lake tradition. Girls only."

Eva got up and happily lost herself in the crowd of dancing women.

It felt good to dance. It felt good to know the song. It felt good to be a part of Blue Lake. Every woman at their table danced her way at some point in the song. They included her in the ritual. She didn't miss Jane as much as she thought she would.

After two glasses of wine, Eva switched to water. She had to drive home. Even though it was so close she could probably walk, even in heels. But her head was swimming and her system was on social overload. She'd been dancing for hours and even though her feet were starting to ache, when Daniel asked her to dance, she said yes before she realized it was a slow song. Damn.

It felt good to be in his arms. Way too good. She pretended it was just for the dance, but she didn't push even a little bit away when he pulled her closer. She put her head on his shoulder. It was just a dance to "Closing Time," an old song, one she'd loved since grade school, before she understood what it felt like to know who she wanted to take her home.

How could it feel so right to be in his arms and how had she not realized that this song was the last song? They'd closed the bar. The hours had passed like minutes.

As everyone headed out to their cars, they were still talking. People shouted goodbyes and a few even said other sweet things to her.

"You're great."

"It's so nice to see Daniel with someone like you."

"Thank you for renovating your cottages!"

"Our town loves you."

One by one, Daniel's friends, and maybe someday her friends, all had something nice to say to her. Meg did one better and grabbed Eva in a tight hug. "I have a feeling we are going to be friends." She whispered into Eva's ear. "So I'll tell you a secret. I'm pregnant." Eva hugged Meg back, closed her eyes, and hoped nobody saw her face in the dark. Then there was a flash. Daniel with his phone camera.

"Send me that one!" Meg said. Getting in the car with her husband and heading home to her growing family.

Daniel walked Eva over to her car. "So did you have a good time?"

"Yes. Thanks. It was fun." She'd been so focused on work that she'd almost forgotten how to be social. She loved dancing.

"I loved dancing with you. Holding you." Daniel held her gaze. She couldn't turn away. She had to quiet her mind. She needed to answer him in a way that would not hurt their friendship but would get her "friends only" message across. This was difficult and confusing. But he didn't want to be "the one"—had in fact stated that he was not the one—so she had to be strong. She was not a one-night stand kind of person. Or even a summer romance type. One by one engines started, headlights flipped on, and a single file of cars left the parking lot, all of them turning left toward town.

Luke gave a quick beep of his horn as he passed them, still there, standing outside her car door. She waved. "How long do you think it will take for Luke to start dating again?"

She'd said it innocently, but Daniel stiffened next to her as if she'd insulted him. "What, you want me to set you two up?"

Oh stars. What an idiot. Didn't he know she was in love with him? She was. In love. With him. Damn it.

"No, I just wondered." She felt tender and a little wounded. "But if I wanted to, you'd do that?" Again, the wrong thing to say. And yet she had to say something so she wouldn't think about what was really on her mind. How could she be so stupid as to fall in love with Daniel?

Daniel didn't answer her. He just walked away and got into his truck. He waited for her to get into her car and take her right turn home before he pulled out and headed the opposite way.

Chapter Nineteen

She answered on the first ring. All business. He wanted to reach the soft interior he knew existed behind her tough outer layer. 'I'm sorry about the way I left things between us at Eddie's last night."

"Oh."

He tried without success to decipher her tone from the single syllable.

"To answer your question from last night, no I do not want to set you up with Luke."

"Okaaaay." Still one syllable but ominously drawn out. He looked at the clock on his kitchen wall. He was due at the site in thirty minutes. Maybe she'd communicate better in person.

"See you in a little while, then."

"See you."

He clicked off his phone. He was not satisfied by two syllables. What he needed was a plan to get her away from work, away from town, away from everyone for a day. He checked his calendar on the way out the door. By his calculations, it was just about doable. If she said yes.

He got to Blue Heaven, as usual, before the rest of the crew showed up. He spotted Eva from the highway inspecting the new sign she'd had commissioned. He parked in the gravel lot and walked back out toward the highway to her.

"Nice."

"Yep."

And they were back to the one syllable conversation again. He only wanted one syllable from her. And that would be her answer to his asking for a date. "I'm sorry about last night."

"You said that already. It's fine. Forget it. Anything else?"

Well, at least there were more syllables.

"Just—I want to ask you something, but you have to promise to say yes."

They walked up the gravel path toward the bungalow together. "Tell me and we'll see."

"I want us to go away for the day. Just get away from all this—"

"You're kidding, right? We're on deadline here."

"I know, but look around. We're ahead of schedule. One day. Just the two of us. That's all I want."

"What would the two of us be doing?"

He realized he didn't have a plan. He had assumed she'd say no. So he improvised.

"I've got a buddy who owns a boat—"

"No boats. I like looking at water, but I get seasick."

He pulled Plan B out of his back pocket. "Okay, we take a couple of bikes and ride Carmella's Curve. Stop on the trail for a picnic." Some of the crew had started to arrive.

"What is Carmella's Curve? And where is it?"

"It's a bike/hike trail that starts in town and goes about twenty miles. We would stop after a mile or so for lunch. You've got to ride it to appreciate it."

"I don't have a bike."

She was not making this easy. "There's a bike rental place in town."

"I hope I'm not going to regret this."

She said yes! Not the actual word, but that was a mere formality.

****

Eva put Lily in charge of the house and Daniel put Bob in charge of the crew. The three of them stood in the kitchen watching Lily tear open a huge box of towels UPS delivered. "I suppose you want these washed too!"

Eva nodded.

"Just do it and then you can get a little beach time in." Eva was too happy to argue with Lily. She was going on a date with the guy she loved. Last night wasn't a real date. Well, maybe a sort of date. But today. He'd put some thought into it and that touched her.

Lily sniffed and took her load into the laundry room.

"When she goes to the beach, you go with her." Eva looked at Bob.

"Okay. I do that anyway."

"If she goes into town, you drive her."

"Well I have to, since she doesn't have a car."

"We'll be home—not too late." She glanced at Daniel, feeling a little shy. "Should I change?" She was wearing sneakers and jeans with a short sleeved top.

"Grab a jacket or a sweatshirt and you'll be set."

They drove into town while Daniel outlined Part 2 of Plan B. "After the bike ride, I want to take you to Amelie's."

Eva heard Amelie's was swank. Beautiful, beachfront, and fancified grass-fed beef. "It's not open yet."

"It's opening tonight. I put a reservation in. Just in case."

"You're so sweet." Eva gushed. She kept trying to hold her feelings in. They'd snuck up on her last night. Ambushed her. She had to work hard to appear casual. She'd just blown it.

Daniel reached over and put his hand over hers, squeezing it. "You're worth it." He parked in front of the bike rental place down a side street Eva had never noticed before. He started to get out of the car, and then stopped and turned to her.

"I really like you, Eva."

"I really like you too."

"I'm not into casual sex. I would never do that. Well, I did some of that, but a long time ago. I'm like you, ready to settle down when I meet the right woman. Just—we aren't there yet. At least give us a chance."

"That's what I'm doing."

"Oh."

Only Daniel would have missed such a large clue. She'd agreed to a bike ride and a picnic. She'd said yes to dinner. What could be clearer? But something in the way he took nothing for granted wrapped her even tighter in the bonds of love.

Jumping on the bikes and riding out of town on a pretty path with the beach on one side and town on the other released her pent-up energy. They couldn't talk much because lots of the time they had to go single file for walkers with their dogs. But when they stopped at a cute little white-washed shanty and ordered their picnic,

Daniel led her to a particular table. She was glad she'd brought a hoodie, because it was close to the water, and she wasn't riding anymore. She thrust her arms into the sleeves. She was starving.

"This table was the one we always sat at when our family went on bike rides. Annual spring tradition. This is the first time I've done this in—well—since they've been gone."

Eva had bitten into her sandwich while he talked and now the lump in her throat made it hard to swallow. She used his gesture from the car and put her hand over his atop the picnic table and squeezed. She kept chewing. After a few minutes of silent munching, she said "So, you've got to be getting excited about Georgia."

"I am. I think. It hasn't been much on my mind since you came to town."

She felt a sweet hit of happy.

"But I've been planning it for years. Got my plane ticket last month."

What was that old song? Something about saying goodbye to love, to happiness. She'd think about all that later. "Well, if you're really serious about seeing how we work out as a couple, I guess next few months will show us both. And let's take it slow. Please." She popped the last bite of her sandwich into her mouth.

"I would never rush you or hurt you, Eva. I feel like the summer won't be enough. Like we'll somehow cross that bridge when we come to it."

"Okay. I'll take a page from your book and stop thinking about your leaving."

"Seize the day." Daniel took his own advice and kissed her. There were other people around, but nothing like the summer crowds. Still, he kept the kiss short and sweet and that was okay with her. Public displays of affection were fine, as long as they didn't cross a specific line drawn in her head. Another plus for Daniel. She kept falling deeper and deeper.

"How long a bike ride can you handle? Because there are some great views along here."

"I have not been on a bike since I was twelve."

"You're kidding?"

"Nope. Guess what they say is true. You never forget."

"So you want to head back?"

"Maybe just a bit further." Spring was greening all around.

The paths were immaculately maintained and around every bend she saw another pretty stretch of water or the glimpse of a perfect Victorian home. The cherry trees had just started blooming and every time she spotted an open blossom she felt blessed.

Chapter Twenty

Eva stared into her closet, not seeing anything. Would Daniel try to make love to her? Would she let him? *Snap out of it!* She needed to focus on the clothes in front of her and not what might happen later. She'd heard all about Amelie's from Jane. What to wear to the classiest, most expensive restaurant in town? She had a slew of city clothes she hadn't even worn here yet. She ignored the little black dresses. She wanted something spring- like, but more formal than a sundress. She pulled a white dress with embroidered sprigs of lavender from the closet and scrutinized it. Sleeveless, but she had a white cardigan. It wasn't quite Memorial Day, but she brought out her white strappy sandals with four-inch heels anyway.

When Daniel picked her up, she was still styling her hair. She took a final glance in the mirror. Good enough. She grabbed her purse and met him in the office.

"You're beautiful," he said. "Great dress."

She bubbled with happiness, and she didn't quite trust it. She was too cautious. *Just be happy already*.

They were seated at the best table in the room, overlooking the water on the left and with a view of the entire restaurant on the right. A full house, but these were quiet diners, mostly older, no children, no sports television noise. She could hear the click of the cutlery as the couple at the next table tucked into their meal. After a brief discussion, Daniel ordered chateaubriand. A single meal, made for two. They drank glasses of mellow cabernet, the wine smooth and rich in her mouth.

While they sipped their first glass of wine and cut into their steaks, they didn't talk much. The beef was so tender she could cut it with a fork and the potatoes melted in her mouth. After the first few bites, Daniel asked her if she missed her job in the city.

"I don't. Detroit advertising revolves around the auto industry. So dull."

"But you stuck with it."

"I had one client I really loved. A big flower chain. That was fun."

"In a few days, Luke can plant flowers and get the lawn in shape for you." Daniel poured wine into their glasses, finishing off the bottle. He said Luke's name casually. He wasn't the jealous type. Another check in his favor.

"Yes, Luke and I already talked about that. Blue Lake is big on petunias, I hear."

"Yep."

They split a dessert that was basically a chocolate bar with caramel and nuts shaped like a tall piece of cake. When they left, it took them ten minutes to get to the door. Daniel stopped at several tables to introduce her. A few of the patrons were from the Fast Eddie's crowd, but most of them were the age his parents would be if they were still alive.

They drove home, and Eva noticed as Daniel pulled into the driveway that both Lily and Bob's lights were on. Lily had probably borrowed Bob's tablet again and Bob was probably watching sports on his laptop. Eva wondered if the two of them had conspired to leave her and Daniel alone.

"Kids are tucked in for the night." Daniel parked and got out to open her door for her. He caught her there, as she came out of the car, in a kiss that made her hold onto him so she wouldn't swoon. *Weak knees are not just an expression*, she thought.

Still kissing her, he closed the door of the car. She wanted the kiss to last forever. She didn't want him to leave her, not now, not ever.

His mouth stayed on her lips but his work-roughened hands roamed her body, from her breasts to her thighs and up above the short hemline of her dress.

"Honey, what if the kids are watching?" She broke the kiss finally when it seemed as if he would undress her and lay her out on the hood of his car.

"Hmmm?" Daniel was still kissing her, pulling at her sweater so he could kiss her shoulder. *Who knew shoulders were erogenous zones?*

It took every ounce of her will to push him a little away. "Let's go inside," she said.

"I thought you'd never ask."

He took her hand and pulled her through the office, through the kitchen, down the hall, into her bedroom. He hadn't turned on any lights. The moon was full and it shined down on them.

"Okay?" He was removing her sweater as he asked.

"Sure," she said, loosening his tie then tearing it from his shirt collar with her teeth. He laughed and caught her hands, bringing them above her head just before her dress followed.

She'd stepped out of her heels. He'd shed his shirt.

She went to work on his belt buckle, laughing with relief that finally the tension that had been building between them for so long was about to find release.

"This feels right. Right?" His leather belt felt smoother than any leather she'd felt before. Like suede.

"Ummm." She kissed him in reply and pushed his shoulders lightly so that he fell onto the bed. He propped himself on his elbows, watching her unzip his pants. Their eyes locked and they both grinned when the tip of his hardened penis sprung free of his boxers.

He broke into a laugh, lay back, and said "Oh, baby."

"Where's the popcorn?"

Eva froze. Lily. From the kitchen. Eva hadn't even heard her come into the bungalow. She looked at Daniel with a promise in her eyes.

"Soon," she said. And then she slipped back into her dress.

****

Luke came early the next day, his truck filled with bags of manure and peat moss, plants and flowers. Eva said she'd be his helper, and so she met him outside in her grubbiest jeans.

"Put me to work, boss," she said.

Eva looked around at her resort. Almost everything was done. This was not a construction site anymore. The airplane addition was buttoned up, only needing paint and shingles. The cottages needed to be fitted out with towels, sheets, dishes. Daniel had finish work to do in the addition. And Luke was here to make the yard look good after spring mud and a construction crew had turned it into a brown gooey mess.

Luke parked by the shed, on the gravel drive where

guests would leave their vehicles. He pulled several large pottery baskets out of the truck and set them on the apron of cement around the shed. Then he eased out several flats of flowers and bags of what amounted to poop and dirt.

"So this will be your job." Luke looked pleased to be giving her flower detail. "While you do that, I'm going to aerate and seed the lawn. It might look a little sparse today but it will fill in quickly. Then I'm going to plant the shrubbery as we decided."

She smiled and shot her arm up in a salute. "Yes sir," she said, before kneeling at the stacked pots, deciding to spread them out. "Oh!" They looked like pottery but they were plastic. That was fine. "What do I put where?"

"Well, you've got your basic fill, the petunias, and the ivy is your spill, this hydrangea is your thrill." Luke handed her the hydrangea, and she smelled it's sweet scent. The smell of summer. "Thrill goes in the middle?"

"Yup. Want me to make one up for you to copy?"

"No, that's fine. I got it." She could work with flowers all day if they all smelled as good as the hydrangea. She couldn't wait until he planted the rose bushes. She loved the scent of roses.

Daniel's car pulled into the drive. He never parked in the guest lot. He got out and came over to where she was kneeling in front of Luke. Daniel shot a quick look from one to the other of them and didn't say anything except "Bud." And then he did a fist bump on Luke's shoulder.

Luke stepped a little away so their positions didn't look quite so suggestive.

Daniel's shoulders relaxed.

"Hey babe," he said, finally acknowledging her. But it was also kind of like he was branding her with the casual "babe." "Going up top. See you for lunch?"

"Yep. I believe Lily is making PBJs for everyone."

"Great." Daniel turned and went into the bungalow.

"That was not an enthusiastic 'great,' "Luke said.

"No. It was not. And I was only kidding. He must be in a mood." Eva knew Daniel was a little jealous. That was okay, even flattering, as long as he kept it to a simmer. Didn't Daniel know she couldn't imagine any other man except him as a romantic partner? Maybe she should tell him. Or better, show him. Soon.

Luke ripped open the bags of soil and manure; whew, not all garden smells were pleasant. He showed her how to properly mix her pots.

She had not even started and her knees already hurt. She sat back on her haunches.

"Well, I'll leave you to it!"

She started with the thrillers. She needed some excitement in her life. Also their sweet smell cut through the manure's assault on her nose.

****

Luke left at lunch, and Eva hoped it wasn't because he could sense Daniel's mood.

"What's eating you?" She and Daniel were alone in the kitchen snacking on grapes. The kids were gone to the hardware in town for a new trowel because Eva had broken Luke's. Daniel made himself a big sandwich, but she wasn't hungry.

"Huh?" He took a huge bite of his Dagwood. Chewed. Swallowed. "What are you talking about?"

"You seem a little, I don't know, pissed off."

"Nope."

"Is it Luke?"

"Nope." He took another bite of his sandwich. She didn't know mouths could open so wide.

"I like Luke, but not the way I like you."

He chewed, nodded his head.

"And last night…"

He finally spoke again. "You don't have to explain about last night. I've been a single dad a long time, don't forget."

"So then it's Luke."

Too late. He'd already taken another bite of his sandwich. He shook his head no and put his hand on hers.

"I'm going to go out there and finish those flower pots."

He nodded, and since he had food in his mouth, she kissed him on the cheek on her way out. "Oh, and Jane invited me to dinner tonight." He didn't respond. Probably still chewing.

****

After a full day of landscaping with Luke, Eva was beat. All she wanted was a long soak in her tub and then lounge on the sofa with the remote until bedtime. But Jane had invited her for dinner, and she'd realized with surprise that it was the first time such an invitation had been issued. Jane always came to her. Or they went out. And she was curious about Jane's house.

She zipped into her best jeans and a beautiful silky black shirt with chiffon sleeves. It felt good to dress up a little bit after mucking about in the yard all day.

She found Jane's house easily enough, a brick ranch with a huge picture window sparkling in the lowering sun and a red front door. Jane came to the door, all smiles, waving Eva inside. Jane motioned toward her apron and flour-dusted hands. "No hugs, don't want to ruin your pretty blouse!"

Eva entered a large foyer area that flowed into the living room space with the big window. Before Eva got more than a glance at the shelter-magazine-perfect décor, Jane clicked across the wood floor, calling for Eva to follow. Since Jane was in heels and skinny red jeans, Eva was glad she'd made an effort beyond her basic wardrobe of jeans and tee.

Jane washed her hands at the sink, untied her apron, and threw it into a room off the kitchen. Jane's kitchen was a gourmet's dream with shiny steel appliances, two ovens, granite countertops, and custom tile work. Two perfect baguettes next to an open bottle of white wine sat on the butcher block center island. "Just took the bread from the oven," Jane said, pouring Eva a glass of wine and topping off her own glass. "Cheers." Jane clinked her crystal against Eva's. The ping hit a sweet high note.

"To friends!" Eva added.

"Okay. The coq au vin is warming in the oven, the salad is assembled in the fridge, as is the chocolate mousse I made earlier. French theme. Like Amelie's."

"Sounds fab." Eva took a sip of her wine. The dinner menu could not be a coincidence. Jane knew about her dinner date with Daniel. Eva took another, larger, sip of her wine, which went straight to her head because she'd skipped lunch and the only food in sight were the two cute loaves of bread. Not so much as a wedge of Brie or even a little tub of butter. Jane made no move to slice the perfectly shaped baguettes.

"I had no idea you baked!" Eva's eyes landed on a new-looking copy of *The Art of French Cooking* closed and propped up on an easel, like a piece of art.

Jane followed Eva's eyes and she giggled.

"Yes. I'm a secret Julia Child clone. I've made every recipe in that book. Twice."

"Impressive!" Eva wanted to grab a loaf of bread and tear a chunk off and cram it in her mouth. She was that hungry. But something stopped her. Wouldn't a real friend just come out with it and admit to being starved?

Jane, despite her perfect hair and manicured nails, had obviously gone to a lot of trouble. Not one pan or whisk or bottle of olive oil in evidence. Everything spotless as a showplace. The round dining table at the other end of the room had been set with a Wedgewood china pattern that picked up the blue and yellow color palette of the room. Even the standing mixer was blue—the stainless steel mixing bowl buffed to a fine sheen and any utensils, like maybe a bread hook, had been tucked out of sight.

"So what's new, girlfriend?" Jane asked, wielding the wine bottle. Eva, astounded, peered into her empty glass.

"Luke came by today and I helped him get the yard in shape."

"Isn't he cute?"

"Yes!" Eva, suddenly giddy and gabby, said "Daniel is so jealous!"

"What? I thought you and Daniel were just friends?"

"I know. We were. We're progressing."

"How far?"

140

Jane drained her wine glass, found the bottle empty and grabbed another from the fridge, which she uncorked with the expertise of a sommelier.

"Just dinner."

"I thought I saw you two biking on Camella's Curve yesterday." Jane's voice was pitched an octave higher than usual.

"We did that too. But we're taking things slow."

Jane had no comment. She turned from Eva to check the stew, took it out of the oven and marched the casserole dish over to the dinner table. Eva hopped up and brought over the bread, which had been resting on a smallish wooden cutting board. She noticed that the loaves had cooled completely. So what was the flour about when she first came to the door?

"Oh, here, give me that." Jane took the bread from Eva and put it back on the island. She pulled a serrated knife from a drawer and started attacking the bread.

"What can I do to help?"

Eva had a sinking feeling that Jane was more than a little drunk. And a bottle of red wine, French burgundy with lots of writing on the label, sat at the dining table, breathing. Fresh red wine glasses nestled next to water goblets.

Eva needed to drive home. She'd already had a glass and a half on an empty stomach. Could she say she was allergic to red wine? Or maybe she'd just had her teeth bleached?

"You can grab the salad out of the fridge," Jane said. Oil and vinegar already sat on the table as well as salt, pepper, and butter.

Eva went to the enormous fridge and opened the door on the right. No salad but an Amelie's take-out box was shoved behind two pretty bowls of pudding.

"Not that side!" Jane snapped, throwing hunks of bread into a plastic container and plopping it on the table, where it didn't quite match up to the elegance of the still life.

Eva opened the other door. A fridge with two doors! Oh, so the chest thing on the bottom was the freezer. Hmm. She pulled out the salad, took off the cling wrap, and joined Jane at the dinner table.

"Well, it looks great." Eva's voice was never more sincere. "Thank you so much." Eva reached for a chunk of bread while Jane filled their wine glasses maybe a third of the way up and proposed another toast.

"To friends!" Jane declared, swirling her wine before tapping Eva's glass.

"Yes, to friends." Eva took a polite sip while noting that the wine was excellent. Nevertheless, she set her glass down and went to work buttering her bread.

She ate with the concentration of a dieter on a binge. "This is all so good. Wonderful." She managed between ravenous bites of chicken and bread. She ignored her salad for now.

"Thanks." Jane was smiling and mellow but not eating much. Eva had so much dinner she wasn't sure where she'd put the mousse.

"We should have music!" Jane clicked a remote and music from high school days roared from discreet speakers somewhere else in the house. Jane turned the volume down a notch even as her head bopped in time to the chords.

"I love this song!" Eva yelled over the music.

"Me too!" Jane got up and began clearing, her plate still almost full. Eva stuffed a buttered bit of bread into her mouth and stood to help. Jane was simply throwing everything into the sink in a messy pile without rinsing off the dishes or taking care with her fine china.

Eva turned on the faucet and started to rinse and stack but Jane turned it off and grabbed Eva's wet hand. "Leave it! Let's dance."

So Eva did. They had fun, just the two of them in Jane's kitchen, rocking out to everything from high school. After an hour, they collapsed and guzzled water.

"This was so great!" Eva said.

"You're my best friend!" Jane replied.

"You're my ONLY friend." But Eva remembered Meg, who might someday become one.

Chapter Twenty-One

The next morning, Eva's bedroom door opened before she'd even gotten out of bed. She was awake. Barely. "Jane?"

"Hi, Eva." Jane sat at the foot of the bed in one of her designer work suits. "Sorry if I woke you."

Eva got up from bed, not caring that she was in slouchy yoga pants and a faded T-shirt. "No, that's okay, thank you so much for last night!" She really wanted to pee and brush her teeth. "Be right back!" She fled into the bathroom. Jane was acting weird. Last night had been a mix of good and bad vibes. Jane had gotten super drunk and didn't want Eva to leave.

Eva finished in the bathroom, but Jane was still sitting on the bed. So Eva went in and sat next to her. "What's wrong, Jane?"

"Did we drink three bottles of wine last night? I can't remember." She picked at the cuticle of her thumb, not looking at Eva.

Eva patted her shoulder. Jane looked at her. "You don't remember?"

"No, but I feel really hung over and, and ashamed. I must have blacked out."

"We did drink quite a bit. But I felt fine to drive home."

"Do you know how much you had?"

Eva thought. "Two white and one red. Then water

and coffee for like, the last two hours." She didn't say that she never finished her second glass of white or that she left most of the red in her glass.

"That's not even a bottle!" Jane dismissed Eva's alcohol consumption like it was nothing. And really, when you've gotta drive home, that's the way it is. "What did I do? Did I say anything mean?"

"No! Of course not. We ate, and danced, and laughed our asses off."

"Whew." Jane visibly exhaled. "That's never happened to me before—where I just forget everything!"

Eva gave Jane a one-armed hug. Jane was a lush. Eva had kind of knew it all along.

"I was nervous, I guess. I never have people over."

Jane didn't have people over and she didn't go out with the old high school gang to Eddie's on Friday nights. Eva wondered why but she didn't want to be intrusive or bring up old wounds.

"Did you take any medicine yesterday?"

"How did you—my meds—let's see—God. I had a Sudafed. I get wicked hay fever every spring."

"There you go. Never mix pills and booze. According to Dr. Oz."

"Oh." Jane's face lightened. "And you're sure I wasn't rude about Daniel or anything?"

"No. We discussed our date at Amelia's. I told you we are taking things slow."

"Yeah, Amelia's. My dad eats there." Then her mouth turned up in a sly grin. "So no sex yet? Am I right?"

Eva shook her head no. She didn't tell Jane that it wasn't for lack of trying.

****

Daniel walked right in when he saw Eva ironing in the office. She had a stack of what looked like fifty pillowcases on the registration counter and was misting the one on the board with something flowery smelling. A few ironed pieces were draped over a chair.

"Hey, babe." He came over and she lifted her mouth to his, which he took as a good sign. He was determined not to ask her how things had gone at Jane's last night.

"So it's pillow day, huh?"

"Yep."

Lily came in from the open door to the private quarters, snagged an ironed pillowcase and shoved a new pillow into it, grunting and moving back into the kitchen where a dozen covered pillows, he now noticed, were stacked on the kitchen table.

"We're a little ahead of Bob with the bed situation. Not a problem. Just, things are happening fast! I feel bad for taking time off."

Daniel hoped she didn't mean taking time off to be with him. Although that's probably what she meant. He didn't ask.

"Where's the list?"

She'd been keeping one, an actual printed out list, with lots of slashes for tasks completed.

"Next to the computer."

He went over to check it. "I can get my stuff done before opening and help. Also, we can call others to help with the domestic end of things if you need them. But really it looks like you've got time."

"Well," she said, "I can iron and talk at the same time. If you're not worried about the airplane."

He got a kick out of her saying "airplane" all the time. He got a kick out of almost everything she said, everything she did, these days.

"Yard looks great."

"Yeah—" She seemed like she wanted to say more, but then she didn't.

"Well, I can see you're busy…"

"Not in any way that would hinder conversation, unless you have stuff to do."

"I have stuff to do." He started up the stairs, then stopped. "How did it go at Jane's last night?"

Eva looked back toward where Lily was stuffing pillowcases and arranged her face into a funny expression, then mouthed something that looked like "later," but he wasn't sure.

"Good," she said.

He went up to finish his room. Well, it was her room, but he thought of it as his room. As usual he got lost in work, sanding the mantel, giving the window frames another coat of clear varnish.

Eva pounded up the stairs.

"Done with the pillow cases already?"

"It took three hours!"

"Oh." Time when by like that when he worked here. Not so at the bank. "So was there something you wanted to tell me about Jane?" He didn't want to ask the question because things were so complicated, but he was curious.

She seemed reluctant to talk. "Looking good," she said, walking around and checking things out but not touching.

"Where's Lily?"

"I think she and Bob went to the beach. You're

right. We've got time. I'm just stressing for no reason. We'll be fine."

If she didn't mention Jane, he wouldn't either.

"Can I ask…is Jane…does Jane…well, does she have a drinking problem?"

Shit. "Like how bad a problem? Define it a bit more. How much wine? One glass? Two? That's not a problem, right? That's all I've seen her drink recently."

"She pretty much killed three bottles last night. And she came over today to apologize and said she blacked out and couldn't remember anything that happened. We had fun. It makes me sad she doesn't remember it. She said it was just a one time thing, that she doesn't have company very often and she was nervous. I think she bought the food, too, but she pretended she'd cooked an elaborate meal."

Double triple shit. He stopped working, put his brush down carefully on top of the varnish can, and got up to stretch. He pulled Eva into his arms. "Jane has had her share of problems in the past. Let's just hope they stay there."

"Like what?" She pulled away to glue her eyes on him.

"What?" He knew he was stalling, but it was better this way. He glanced away from her stare. "Nothing. Stupid high school stuff."

Eva's face relaxed and she put her head on his shoulder. Let him hold her. They had a lot to accomplish today so he knew this was a short respite, but it was oh so sweet. And Jane. Well, he was going to forget all about Jane and her problems. She wasn't his problem anymore.

"You need to expand your circle of friends."

He felt her nod her head against his chest. "I like Meg."

"And you'll like the others too."

"They all have families. Husbands and kids."

Daniel felt himself tense up and made an effort to relax. "Not everyone. And who says you can't be friends with married people?"

"It's like being friends with a millionaire. Really hard."

He was a millionaire. He'd never mentioned it. There were tons of millionaires. It was the billionaires who had cachet now. Millionaires? Dime a dozen.

"I love new babies. If I become friends with Meg, who I like so much, I would be holding her new baby. And then I'd want one for myself."

"What, no daddy?" He tried to tease her out of her mood.

"Yes." She pulled away and socked him on the arm.

"Honey, Meg and Steve met in elementary school. They went steady starting in sixth grade. They never broke up once."

She let out a big sigh. "I know. You're right. I just feel like I wasted my twenties on Marcus."

"But that was good, because now you have me."

She smiled a sad smile. "Yes. Now I have you."

"All finished with your ironing?"

"All done. There are pillows everywhere."

He decided just like that. He was done for the day, too. The sun was going down. The light wasn't right. And he had her here now. All her attention focused on him. It felt good.

"Got any plans for tonight?"

"No. You?"

"Well—I was hoping to spend it with you." He was hoping for a whole lot more, but tonight was not about that. Tonight should be him showing her how much he cared. Trouble was, he couldn't think of a date type thing they had not already done. Dinner, movies, bike ride, picnic, another dinner. There had to be something special.

Then he thought of it. "I'm not sure this will work. The wind has kicked up a bit. He looked at the sky. No clouds. That was good. The tide churned as dusk settled in.

Sounds from television and teenagers floated up the steps. He could take her to his house instead of the other thing, but the last time she was there they'd been in bed within ten minutes. She'd asked him to take things slow. He wanted to honor that promise, no matter how difficult it was to keep.

****

Daniel was being very secretive. Still, Eva wanted Lily to know they were going out. "We'll be back in an hour or so. I have my cell if you need me."

"Yes, mom," Lily teased.

Daniel not telling her where they were going, even once they were in his car and on the way down the road, didn't bother her. Wherever he was, that's where she wanted to be. They drove out of town, past the high school. He turned down an unpaved road, wooded on both sides of the path. Branches hit the windshield but Daniel kept driving, slowly now on the narrow path. Dusk drew in and darkness settled. The trees looked black.

Daniel stopped when they came to a clearing with

an old barn on one side, practically falling apart. The roof had peeled off. In the glare of the car's headlights, she saw how it hung down on one side of the building, like a giant head of unruly hair.

Daniel cut the lights and grabbed a flashlight from his glove box. They got out, and guided by the flashlight, she followed him around the car. He opened the trunk and handed her a blanket.

He turned the light toward the path and when she didn't move he said, "Come on!" He took her hand and they walked up to the barn by the light of the beam. When she stopped in front of the decrepit building, he tugged her hand. "Let's go."

"What? In there?"

"Yep. It's great. You'll see."

"But why?" Her arms were covered in goose bumps and she let his hand go, clumsily zipping up her hoodie while holding a blanket.

The flashlight was big and shined a powerful light. Daniel grabbed her hand again and pulled her toward the old building.

She wanted to know what the hell he was up to, but when she asked again, he said "You trust me, right?"

"Of course."

"Then come on."

Once they were inside the barn, he shined the light around the big empty space.

"See? Nothing to fear."

"I wasn't afraid." But she was, just a little bit, when Daniel's light shone on a set of stairs. "Stair steps seem to be an essential component of our relationship." She said it to calm herself down. She hoped he wasn't planning some middle school horror monster joke.

151

Daniel laughed low, as if not to disturb whatever creatures lurked above. He guided her to the stairs and took the first step.

"No. Really? We're going up?"

"Perfectly safe. School kids come here all the time to drink beer, smoke cigarettes, and make out."

She giggled exactly as if she were a school girl. It was part parody and part real. Daniel made her feel that way. So young and carefree.

"It's perfectly legal for us to do those things in more comfortable places." Despite the complaint, she followed him up to the roofless room on top of the barn.

Again, he shined his light around the four walls. A discarded blanket. A few empty beer cans. Daniel picked a spot in the center of the room to lay down the blanket. She stood there, unwilling to lay down in case a mouse or a bat or something decided it wanted to make a nest in her hair.

"Come on, lay next to me. The stars are amazing tonight!"

So she lay down next to him, using her purse as a pillow against creeping creatures. Then she gazed up at the sky. It left her breathless. Here was a world, a galaxy, a universe, all around them. It made her feel very small but also a part of the largeness. Now scientists talked about multiverses. Universe after universe, reaching out toward infinity.

"Where's the moon?"

"New moon tonight."

"I never knew what that meant."

"It's because we see moonlight, which is really a reflection of the sun off the moon's surface. The moon doesn't really glow. It orbits around our planet. The moon, sun, and earth get into new patterns of orbit. When sunlight is blocked from the moon, we say "new moon."

"A friend of mine always did a new moon ceremony. Where she let the old go and blessed whatever new was entering her life."

Then they were silent for a time, star-gazing, making their own new moon beginning.

"Thank you," she finally said, turning her body on its side, facing him. "This is lovely." She doubted high school kids watched the stars in here, but maybe some did. Daniel turned his body to hers, closed her in his arms, and kissed her. Her fingertips smoothed through his hair and she opened her mouth to his. She could kiss him until the next new moon.

He pulled back but kept his arms round her. He gazed at her like she was a star. He brushed her cheek.

"You're so beautiful."

She wasn't, but it was a sweet thing to say, and she knew he meant it. She leaned in for another kiss. His hands didn't roam her body, he gave everything to the kiss. His body touched hers from head to toe, so she knew he wanted to make love, or his body certainly did, and yet, he held back. He was going slow, as she'd asked.

His kiss made her dizzy with desire, but then they heard a car door slam, whispers, and giggles stumbling up the stairs. They took a final look at the star studded sky, then rolled up the blanket and descended back to earth.

Four kids, not much younger than Lily, piled in the doorway like a litter of puppies. One guy held a Bic lighter high as if saluting his favorite band.

"Oh, hey, man, sorry." Bic guy flicked off his light for a second, then relit it.

"You guys want a beer?" The other guy held out a can while the girls giggled and whispered to each other with their hands over their mouths.

"No, thanks." Daniel declined the beer. "We're just leaving."

"Later," the beer guy said.

Eva was okay with the kids interrupting them. She wanted her first time with Daniel to be special. On a soft mattress. But this had been a bit of fun, like high school, when she and her love of the moment and all their friends tried to find a place to be alone and act like adults when they all lived with their parents. That's what Daniel had been up to tonight. He wanted them to have a high school experience. He was building memories. But what memories was she creating for him? She needed to seriously up her game.

****

Eva stood outside in the sunshine, a box of kitchen things in various shades of blue for Blueberry Cottage in her arms, watching Bob stripping and painting headboards. Every frame had been assembled, every mattress delivered. Since all the structural work was finished, she and Lily had been adding little touches, filling the tiny kitchenette cupboards, adding toiletries to the bathroom cabinets.

She was in a great mood despite the frustrating interruptions she and Daniel seemed to suffer every time they were getting to that place. The ultimate destination for two people in love. Not that he'd said he loved her. She hadn't said it either, but she'd thought it. Maybe he was thinking it, too. Making love would happen at the right time, but last night, Lily had decided to sleep on the sofa bed in the living room. Daniel handled his exit discreetly, flushing the toilet and coming down the hall to say goodnight to both Eva and Lily.

Lily's room in the bungalow was painted and she had already appropriated the best of the headboards Bob had been working on for herself, a curving iron piece that Bob had lovingly removed the rust from and painted a pretty off-white to match Lily's walls.

Lily kept her cottage, too, so Eva never knew exactly where the girl was sleeping, but that would all be over soon. In a little over a week's time, her first guests would arrive, and Lily would be in the bungalow for good. This thought didn't bother Eva like it once would have.

She went into Blueberry and arranged the tea pot and mismatched china cups and plates, then went back to the office. She turned on her laptop, intending to work on the Bryman House website, when she gave in to temptation and checked her email.

Marcus. What the hell. Curious, she opened the message.

"Heard about your little venture," he wrote. "My news? Moving to New York next week to take charge of a boutique agency."

No *Good luck*, no *Sorry*, no *It wasn't you it was me*.

Damn him. She clicked off email and into her bank account. Her work crew had been paid and thanked. Now it was just Daniel and Bob doing finish carpentry upstairs and the occasional odd job. Bob refused to take a paycheck anymore, because he split his time between

Bryman House and Blue Heaven, and he was just here "hanging out" and "helping Daniel."

It was probably a good thing, because she only had about $10,000 left, and she needed that as an emergency fund. It was less than Suze Orman said you needed, and until paying guests arrived, she'd be buying groceries with it.

With the way Bob ate, next time he offered, she'd let Daniel pay for the pizza. Daniel. He'd made her forget about this venture. She needed to focus on her business and be very careful with her money.

"You should have a party," Jane said, coming into the office. Eva hadn't even heard her car come up the driveway. She turned off her laptop and got up to greet her friend.

"Very nice," Jane said, running her hand along the refinished wood counter, checking out the gleaming bannister and the curved staircase, the newly papered walls, the little sitting area Eva had arranged just that morning.

"A party?"

"He's almost finished, right?" Jane pointed upstairs. "Invite the town. It would be a good way to thank the crew, and let their families see what they've been doing for the past six weeks."

"I would, but I'm on a budget here," Eva confessed.

"You'll be fine," Jane assured her. "You're fully booked June, July and August. You've even got the fall leaf peepers booking early."

Eva knew Jane was right. Everything had been done according to plan. Everything would work out.

"So like an open house? With soft drinks and

cookies?" She would love to see Meg again. Luke and the others, too.

"Potato salad and burgers, maybe beer and wine." Jane added to Eva's modest list.

Eva was happy to do more to thank her crew. Inviting the town would be good for business and for her personal life. But what would a bash like that cost?

"It'll be fine. Everyone brings a side dish, Eddie donates a keg, you get the rest at Costco."

Eva loved the idea. "Okay."

****

Daniel stopped sanding the window sash when Eva came up and stood in the middle of the empty room. He wanted to hug her she looked so worried. He wanted to tell her everything would be okay. He wanted to tell her to please not start seeing Luke after he left town.

"What is it?"

"Nothing. Really."

"It's something. You never just come up here. You hate sanding grit."

"Jane thinks I should have an open house. For the entire town."

"And this has you worried because?"

"I'm trying to watch my budget. I mean, I really do want to do this, but should I? Maybe I should wait until Labor Day and hold a 'Thank You' barbecue instead."

"You'll be fine," Daniel said. "You know how the video has been getting crazy hits? Well, we can get my buddy to videotape the Open House. Imagine if every person in Blue Lake sent the link to the video to every one of their family members who live downstate or even out of state? You'll be booked YEARS in advance."

She sat on the hearth.

Daniel sat next to her. He reached over and put one hand on her knee.

"I'm sorry," he said. He wasn't sure why he said it. To her, it might seem like it came out of nowhere, but she was all he could think about. How sweet she was. How hard she worked. How stupid the guy who dumped her was. How, for him, she was the right woman at the wrong time.

"Sorry for what?"

"Us. Me leaving town instead of settling down to raise babies like Meg and Steve."

She was so still next to him, he knew he'd hit a nerve. He was used to her always being in motion.

"What smells so good in here?" she said, avoiding the subject again. He had no clue how to get through to her. He could feel their connection, why couldn't she?

"It's the apple wood."

"It's not even lit."

"I know. Imagine how it will be with a fire going." Daniel decided to try out the fireplace. After all, he had to know if the room was going to smoke up before the open house. He drew a pack of matches from his pocket and lit the kindling he'd laid underneath the apple wood.

"Why are we lighting a fire? Why are we chatting about old times, before we even knew each other? We have so much to do before the Open House!"

Daniel grabbed Eva's hand as she started to rise from the hearth.

"I want to see if the chimney draws right," he said. "And we can take five minutes to talk."

"About what? Us? Can we please just wait to go

any more public than we already are until after the opening? I feel like everything is moving so fast. It's finally here."

Daniel didn't know where else to go with this. Why couldn't they just date openly and see where it went once they were in it? How did you say that to a woman without sounding like she was being evaluated?

She squinted.

"Do you see smoke hovering up there around the light fixture?"

"No." Daniel felt frustrated but he also could sense the pressure Eva was under. So okay, he'd back off for a few days.

"I thought we were in love," she said, out of nowhere.

Daniel felt a jolt of electricity, fear or excitement, maybe a combination of the two, until he realized she wasn't talking about the two of them, but about the other guy, the older one from her past.

"You're helping me, like he did. You're showing me the ropes. You're giving me free labor and materials."

"It's a trade. You're going to help me with the museum."

"Still. It feels the same."

"And that's bad because?"

"Because it ended."

She wasn't looking at him, but at the flames of the fire.

He thought about that. So, she wanted a guarantee. Talking about Georgia and how he couldn't wait to get out of town had not helped his case. Of course that would bother her. She was not the hook-up type. She was the dive right in and do it, get married and have kids, type.

And then he remembered how he'd told her his parenting days were over. Right before he'd said that, she'd been warm and open. The next day she told him he couldn't kiss her anymore. She'd made the excuse about work, but now he got it. He saw clearly who she was and what she needed. The question was, did he want to step up and give it to her?

Chapter Twenty-Two

Eva had just confessed her feelings about Marcus to Daniel when Jane came up the stairs, carrying a bottle of wine in one hand and three glasses in the other. He probably didn't understand what she'd been talking about. He'd gone silent in the way men did when they were clueless.

"This is gorgeous," Jane said. Eva loved Jane. She'd become her best friend in such a short time. She cared about Daniel too, but he wouldn't always be here.

Looking from Jane to Daniel, Eva wondered about their shared past. They seemed so casual around each other. You'd never know they'd been lovers, that they'd raised Bob together. At least according to Jane.

She noticed their interactions as Daniel accepted Jane's glass of wine, pointing out the features of the room to her. Like old friends. Like family members. Not like lovers at all. Why did she keep looking for signs that were not there?

She studied them for a few minutes. Did Jane touch Daniel's arm out of friendship or unrequited love? Did Daniel use his shorthand way of talking to Jane because they grew up together or because he trusted her to understand his reference points?

Just when Eva was starting to think that the two of them seemed so cozy and oblivious to her, Jane turned and grinned. "So, what's the plan for the Open House?

How can I help?"

Daniel asked if anyone wanted to split a pizza.

"Eva and I were going over to Fast Eddie's for burgers," Jane said.

"What's Bob doing?"

"He and Lily had their eyes on a box of macaroni and cheese in the pantry," Eva said.

"You can join us," Eva finally said, when Jane didn't.

"No, no, that's okay. I want to finish sanding the mantel and get a coat of stain on her."

Jane looked at Eva and they both laughed.

"What?" Daniel wanted to know.

"You referred to the mantel as 'she' like it was alive," Eva said.

"Like 'she' was your girlfriend," Jane teased.

"Just go have dinner. You can bring me back a carry out. If that's not too much trouble."

"No trouble," Jane and Eva said at the same time.

****

Eva and Lily had spent the day at the Costco in Port Huron, buying supplies for the Open House. Would four cases of wine would be enough? Eddie from the bar was going to donate a keg of beer. He also said he'd man the tap. One more worry Eva could cross off her list. She hadn't known how she'd keep the teenagers from drinking.

So far, the RSVPs were up to 200. Jane said more people would show up, not bothering to RSVP, or not knowing that it was even required. Not everyone had a computer, not everyone had a cell phone. And Open House did sort of mean "come whenever if" or so Jane explained to Eva.

She'd pulled a couple thousand out of the bank for food and paper products. Then worried over her bank balance. No need, she'd told herself, adding up the total for her first week's renters. Still, a part of her would not be happy until she'd proved she could repay that loan not by reservations, but by cash in hand.

They came home with a loaded down car and started unpacking. Bob helped, telling her he had finished staining the gazebo, a gift from the Bryman brothers. Eva had of course argued that the gazebo gift was entirely unnecessary, but they'd insisted, and she'd felt churlish about saying no so she finally accepted it with as good grace as she could muster. It was just that they were doing so much for her. It never ended. But she had to admit, the gazebo would be a great little place to sit with a summer drink, looking over the water without going down to the beach.

Right now it sat under a huge canvas tent, just in case of rain. The side that was open to the water had been screened with canvas, and if it actually did rain, Bob could lash the other three canvas sides into place.

"I'll take the canvas down in the morning if the sun is out," Bob said. Eva had no doubt that the sun would shine down on her party.

Bob helped Lily get the rest of the party supplies unloaded and stored. He'd offered to man the barbecue at the Open House, and had asked for a certain kind of grilling charcoal, which they'd found, so he was happy.

Eva went to the street to get her mail and saw the stack of dreaded credit card bills.

She opened the bill that said "IMPORTANT INFORMATION ABOUT YOUR ACCOUNT" on the outside of the envelope first. It said her interest rate had been doubled. Another card that had guaranteed zero percent interest for a year had raised her rate to 18%. She quickly did some numbers in her head. She hadn't counted on the extra expense of these interest rates. She felt like she was drowning. She knew this was happening to people all over the country, but she couldn't believe it had happened to her. Or that she'd let it.

"What would Marcus do?" She wondered. They'd had plenty of experience with going over budget on a campaign and he'd always found a creative way to solve problems.

One thing she knew for sure is that he would not let his confidence waver for one second. All she needed was confidence in the plan unfolding as it should. Her vacationers would come, they would pay, she would be solvent. Maybe she should take that on faith and pay a couple of these cards off with her emergency savings. She'd already dipped into it for the party. 18% would add up quickly over the winter months, when she had no revenue coming in.

She went online and transferred her savings to checking, but held off writing the checks. She still had a little bit of cash in there and some time before the bills came due. Everything would be fine. She would have faith in herself and in the universe. What could go wrong now with less than a week until opening day of the new Blue Heaven?

****

The morning of the Open House, Eva arranged the finishing touches in the addition. Happy and excited, she also felt a little ache inside she couldn't quite place. Probably just pre-party nerves. There would be so many people she didn't know. She knew Meg and Luke and the rest of the people from Eddie's. She knew the guys on the renovation crew, Lois the vet, plus Eddie from the bar and the lady who owned the antique store. She was beginning to feel part of a community, even if she couldn't remember everyone's name.

The mantel had been bare while the stain dried, but now she arranged family photos there. She missed her folks. Even though she spoke to her mom on the phone every week, it wasn't the same. She admired her walls, their golden yellow paint cheered her. A light green sectional with clean lines that could easily seat twelve reflected the leaves of the trees outside the many windows. She didn't have anything covering the windows at all, because Daniel had done such an incredible job on the wood framing them and the view from every angle of nature was better than any textile could provide.

Daniel. How would they behave today around the entire town? As a couple or still remain quietly seeing each other? She knew he wanted them to be open about their relationship and realized, as she moved a picture frame an inch to the left, that she wanted that, too.

The room looked perfect to her eyes but what would other people think? She picked up and rearranged a fat aqua urn, set a large bowl of oranges on the coffee table. Her eyes rested on Mama, taking a well-deserved break from the kittens on a rust-colored throw puddled on a chaise lounge. Eva angled a guitar she'd bought for $5 next to the cat. A perfect still life.

Maybe too perfect. She took one orange out of the bowl and set it next to a pair of candlesticks holding tall amber colored candles. No more fussing. That was it.

Everything was done. If she was nervous today, what would it be like when the magazine came knocking? Daniel had given her the news yesterday. A writer and photographer would be arriving next week on Monday to do a feature on Bryman and Blue Lake. It was a dream come true for Daniel, and from a marketing standpoint, for her business, too.

She took one final glance around the room, hoping Daniel liked her finishing touches. If he approved, it almost didn't matter what anybody else thought. He had not seen it since he'd helped her, Bob, and Lily arrange the heavy pieces delivered yesterday. She'd practically lived up here since then.

Daniel had done so much for her, she wished she'd thought of a really good surprise for him. Her wheels were turning as she went downstairs to make sure everything there was okay. Her showplace rooms were the office with the new curving bannister and the living room. The kitchen still looked the same, tiny but cheery. She'd have to show her bedroom, but had installed a baby gate so people knew not to go into it, just take a peek at the cavorting kittens. They were her excuse for the baby gate, a bit of advice from Jane, who said she'd have people sitting all over her bed unless she made it off limits.

Eva sorted out the house as best she could, and even came up with what she hoped would be a neat surprise for Daniel. She thought about it as she cleaned up after herself in the bathroom. She thought about it as she put on jeans and a casual tunic. She didn't think she'd get cold, but because of the plan, she changed from her white tunic to a deep blue one. How would she fit the surprise into the constant activity of hostess? She knew Daniel's surprise would not make her cold, but she hung a sweater over her office chair just to be safe.

She checked the computer. A few more RSVPs. Another reservation for fall.

Jane and Daniel came in together while Eva was still in the office.

"Looks like rain," Jane said.

Eva winked at Daniel. That was it for now. But later, after the guests arrived...well, she just hoped he'd be happy.

Chapter Twenty-Three

"No way." Eva put her sexy plan out of her mind to disagree with Jane about the rain, pointing to the patch of sunshine on her patterned rug. She clicked off her website and shut the computer down. She took the various papers all over her desk and gathered them up into a tidy sheaf before stashing them in a drawer. Then she came out from behind the registration counter to join her friends.

"If it rains, people can use the tent. We'll control the number of folks touring the place."

"Nobody's going in MY cottage or my room." Lily carried a baby gate as she stomped in behind Bob.

Eva shrugged. Lily was entitled to her privacy, while Bob had been stoic about returning to live with Daniel.

Things were changing. First the noisy crew left, now Bob would be leaving tonight, and Lily would officially move into the bungalow with Eva. Then the guests would descend. The new idea she'd come up with to surprise Daniel in the midst of all these strangers terrified and elated her at the same time.

Frank was the first guest after her friends to arrive. His wife smiled so wide her face almost cracked as she handed Eva a huge Tupperware container of fruit salad. His kids, teenagers, were drawn immediately to the beach. Eva and Jane had been right about the weather.

It was still warm and sunny, but there were dark clouds on the horizon.

Maybe people would notice the impending showers and show up earlier rather than later.

A guy from the crew came next, with his wife, who carried a Bible in her hand.

"Vera here wants to say a blessing over your place," he said, eyeing the keg of beer that Eddie was priming.

He left Eva alone with Vera, even though Eva could see that she was not going to be alone, not really, for many more hours. People were pouring into her property like they poured out of church on Sunday morning.

"I do hope you'll succeed here," Vera said piously, "even though I'm unsure whether the Lord really approves of the name of this place."

"That was the name it had before I owned it," Eva said.

"I know," said Vera, pointedly. But then someone else came up, a guy from the cottage crew. He introduced his wife and kids and cousins and uncle.

A few hours later, which had passed like minutes, Eva was weary but relieved. Her new neighbors had welcomed her and she felt good about that. She just had a minute to sneak into the bathroom and call her mother. She'd figured out what was missing in her perfect house. Her family.

"Mom, you have to come up here and see this place," Eva said, for the hundredth time.

"I saw it online, honey. Your cousin Marcie sent me the link."

"Marcie!" Eva let that go for the moment. "I didn't

know you had a computer!"

"I had to get one. My friend Ernst has one with a little camera and he talks to his grandkids that way."

"Oh, a webcam. Good idea. Let's do that. Who is Ernst?"

"He's my neighbor, dear. We're not having sex, if that's what you're thinking."

Eva hadn't been thinking any such thing. She looked in the mirror and realized she'd forgotten to put on make up this morning. Which is probably why all the women were so friendly. She was for sure no competition. She grabbed a mascara wand from the basket of make up under the sink, hesitated, and snagged her blusher, too.

"Okay, well, Mom. Back to Marcie. I didn't know you talked to her."

"Yes, that was your father's fight. When he died, the fight died with him, bless his heart."

Eva felt a sense of calm she'd been missing since she'd started this project. She'd gotten a couple of her cousins' email addresses off the internet and sent them the link to Blue Heaven. Just in case they might be interested in seeing their childhood summer home again. She hadn't heard back from any of them, and that stung, but apparently at least Marcie had seen the website.

Someone knocked on the door. "Mom, I have to go. I'm having a party."

"Oh, I'm glad you're making friends, dear."

Eva was glad, too. This was a small town and she intended to spend the rest of her life here, so it would be good if she liked the people.

She opened the door. Jane stood there.

"Oh, hey you."

"Hey you, too." They grinned at each other like fools. She'd never have been able to do any of this without Jane's help. From the first day, Jane had been there for her, even way back when Daniel wasn't.

"Thank you," she told Jane.

"For what? Putting ranch dressing in plastic shot glasses and sticking in a few raw veggies?"

"No, for this. For everything. You are the person who started everything in motion. I can't thank you enough."

"It was nothing," Jane said. "Wait for me, I want to ask you something."

So Eva went into the kitchen and talked with people until Jane joined her.

"Let's go sit on the porch," Eva said. Jane laughed, and in a minute Eva knew why. The big covered porch was strictly standing room only. But that was okay.

"What did you want to ask?" Eva said, going outside, heading for the shed, where her plan for Daniel was ready to spring.

"Just, well. I wondered about you and Daniel." God, the girl had ESP.

"Not much to tell. We're taking it slow." Eva wasn't going to tell anyone, not even Jane, what she had planned.

"I know, I know, but I keep getting a bad vibe."

Eva shook her head no. "You worry too much."

Just then Daniel came up behind her and Eva figured it was now or never. She took him by the hand, pulled him closer to the shed, looked back at Jane, and winked.

"What? Where are we going? I wanted to introduce

you to…"

She pulled open the shed door a crack with the stealth of a top notch sleuth. She went in sideways, pulling Daniel after her. It was dark, but she didn't turn on the light. Daniel stopped protesting even before she kissed him.

She relaxed into an embrace that had become her main source of comfort. Even joy. It felt like an old song her mother had loved, something about fading into your lover. Not that he was yet. And this was not the place for that. But soon.

After their skin had connected through their clothes and it truly felt as if she'd fade into him, Daniel moved his lip an inch from her own. "What are you up to?"

"Nothing," she answered back. "Just kissing you." And she did. She planned to kiss him until someone noticed one or both of them were missing from the party. If things went her way, that would be at least an hour from now.

The shed door banged. Damn. Way too soon.

"What are you guys doing in there?" Jane whispered.

"Shhh. Nothing. Kissing." Eva laid her head on Daniel's flannel shirted shoulder. "Go away for awhile."

Jane didn't say anything else, but someone noticed her there and soon several voices could be heard. Busted. But that had been her plan all along. Now it just needed someone opening the door and catching them in the act. Well, the act of kissing.

Jane was busy trying to divert people from the shed. "Nobody. It's nothing. Let's get you a drink!" But it didn't work. Lily had noticed that both Eva and

Daniel were missing.

"They're in there!"

"What? Who?"

"Come on, guys. Out with it or I'm coming in." Lily again.

Eva didn't move from her spot in Daniel's arms. She kissed him again. He might be confused by her willingness to be caught, but he kissed her right back just the same.

A few minutes later a real ruckus had started outside the shed.

"Hope you have all your clothes on!" Bob said, then opened the shed door. Eva and Daniel continued to kiss amid a chorus of glee and a few less tasteful remarks.

"I knew you two were doing it!" Frank said.

"Young love," said an older woman Eva didn't know.

They broke off their kiss and Eva held Daniel's hand as they faced the world. Well, at least one little piece of it.

"Doing what?" Daniel asked. "I didn't know there was a law against kissing a pretty girl." They walked out of the shed and he raised the hand he held and kissed her like an old-fashioned gentleman.

Eva looked around, but she didn't see Jane. She hoped her friend wasn't offended because she hadn't clued her in on the shed secret.

A very loud "Meow" sounded from the shed rafters as Papa cat protested the noise in his cozy abode. Bob had built him a little door so that he had free access at all times and, after jumping down from his perch, he ignored it and twisted out among the crowd, loudly meowing hellos to everyone. Papa was the talker in the cat family.

Everyone pelted them with questions and comments all at once.

"We've been seeing each other a while," Daniel said. "Just taking it slow."

"Since when have you ever taken anything slow?" Luke shouted from the back of the crowd. Everyone laughed and somebody popped a champagne cork. That had not been part of her plan, but she liked it. Bob came through and handed Eva and Daniel each a glass. A real flute. Probably borrowed from Daniel's house because Eva had no flutes. Everyone else raised their paper cups as Bob said "Here's to Eva and Daniel for finally admitting what everybody already knew!"

Daniel looked into her eyes as they clinked glasses. "You are really something," he said so only she could hear.

"I thought it was time to properly announce our being a couple."

"Wasn't anything proper about that." Daniel laughed and turned to a few of his buddies who were mercilessly teasing him.

Eva heard a voice from her past. It couldn't be. Lord, say it wasn't so.

"Peanut!" She turned around and there was Marcus, holding yet another bottle of champagne in one hand and a dozen yellow roses in the other.

****

"It's my fault. I sent out a massive email announcing the opening of Blue Heaven and he was likely on my list." Eva whispered to Jane as the party swirled around them and Daniel, of all people, gave

Marcus a tour of the house. Marcus brought the rain, which thinned the crowd somewhat, although there were still small knots of folks in the house and under the beer tent.

Jane and Eva sat in the gazebo. Watching it rain. Jane knew the Marcus story. There was nothing to say, so they watched the rain pelt into the churning gray water of Lake Huron.

"Guess I should go rescue Daniel," Eva said.

"You sure surprised everyone with that shed trick."

"I just wanted everyone to know we're a couple."

"Everyone except me."

"You knew. I told you. Said we were taking it slow."

Jane pursed her lips.

"Hey, sorry if you felt excluded." Eva got up from her seat. "I need to change into dry clothes and see what the hell Marcus is up to."

"I'm coming." Jane put on her game face and pulled a plastic garbage bag from her jeans pocket. They began loading it with dirty paper plates and plastic cups and napkins. By the time they made it back to the house they were both soaked, but the bag was full, they were friends again and the yard was tidy.

The beer tent buzzed with old timers from the bar. Not only the three wise men, whose names she could never remember, there were a dozen or so more wizened souls, elbows on picnic tables, grinning at her, saying her daddy would be proud. That she and Daniel were made for each other. She thanked them and double checked to make sure none of the kids were sneaking beer. They weren't. No kids in the house either, which meant they'd probably left. Or maybe they were in the cottages. With alcohol.

"If you happen to run into Marcus and Daniel, tell them I'll be right there. I want to lock up the cottages," Eva said to Jane.

Nobody in Peach, Watermelon, Kiwi, or Blueberry. Eva locked up after surveying the premises. She and Lily would have to clean in the morning, but they'd expected that. No irreparable damage, which is what she'd really been worried about. The other two cottages, Cherry and Coconut were still Bob's and Lily's cottages, at least for tonight.

Both were occupied, music and laughter coming from inside, so Eva decided to let them carry on. She hoped they weren't drinking, but she was not cut out to police the world of teens, nor was she a parent. You had to grow into parenthood, she thought, wondering about Daniel, what he would do right now. She decided to ask him. Maybe he'd invade their space and check for contraband for her.

The house was emptying out, at least the main floor. Meg and Steve had left awhile ago with most of Daniel's friends. A few people sat in the living room, looking out at the rain and sipping wine.

Four or five women, wives of the crew who took a touching pride in their project, were putting away food and cleaning up party damage in the kitchen.

"Thanks so much." Another of the wives had gone out to the porch with a large garbage bag. "But you don't have to do this."

"Look at you! Soaked to the bone," Luke's mom— was her name Wanda?—said. "We don't mind a bit. Go on and get into some dry clothes. Jane already borrowed a pair of your jeans and a T-shirt."

Eva craved a warm shower and her fuzzy robe and slippers, but that would be rude.

"Thanks, then," she said, smiling at them before taking the baby gate down and slipping into her bedroom to change. She grabbed a clean towel from the hallway linen closet to dry her hair. Then she spent a few minutes combing it. After she smoothed on a coat of clear lip gloss and washed the mascara from under her eyes, she couldn't stall anymore. She went upstairs to face her doom.

The room smelled like apple wood. Lamps glowed warmly in the darkening space and around her sectional, a half full bottle of wine rested in a cloth napkin on the coffee table. Jane, Daniel, and Marcus sat there, looking like the best of friends.

The roses Marcus brought, her favorite, were spread out in all their splendor in a cut crystal vase she didn't remember owning. Marcus, no doubt, had brought it along, the better to display his gift. She had to admit that the beautiful crystal against the rustic dark wood was a gorgeous pairing, although the bowl of oranges she'd so carefully arranged that morning had disappeared. Amazingly, nobody was upstairs but the four of them.

Daniel smiled at her as she came into the room.

Jane and Marcus were involved in a discussion of the best area of Manhattan for apartment hunting.

Daniel got up and came over to pull her to the seat next to his. He handed her a clean wine glass and poured Chardonnay into it as Jane and Marcus looked over, both of them laughing at something Marcus had just said.

"Okay I borrowed some togs?" Jane asked.

"Sure."

"You've got more jeans than I do."

"And probably in more sizes," Eva laughed. "Except you're so tall."

"I'm calling them capris," Jane said, stretching out her long leg to show bare inches above her ankle.

The guys looked mildly befuddled, but when nobody spoke for a minute, Marcus came into the breach smoothly saying, "You done good, Peanut." She'd never liked the pet name. At five-foot-three, she wanted to forget she was shorter than the average girl. "Thanks," she said, smiling painfully. Glad that Daniel and Jane didn't remark on the Peanut moniker.

"If I weren't moving to New York, I'd come here myself this summer," he said. "I was so impressed with the video online."

Eva smiled her gratitude at Daniel, hoping today's video wouldn't feature a single frame with Marcus in it.

Again the room fell silent, but she didn't feel like she needed to fill it. She had nothing left to say to Marcus, and both Jane and Daniel knew the story.

The three of them curled up cozy and at home, Marcus the odd man out. Until he picked up the guitar. He tuned it for a few minutes, even though she'd had it restrung and tuned, then started plunking out the opening to an old punk anthem. He even got that high note right where you have to press your pinky and twist it to make the note tremble.

Showing off.

He segued into more of his idea of what kids listened to, except those songs weren't new anymore. He riffed a few notes before moving on to something else, but she knew his songbook by heart.

Marcus played the piano, and didn't fool much with the guitar, except when he was trying to impress the younger generation.

Like now.

Chapter Twenty-Four

Eva ignored Marcus and turned to Daniel.

"Do you think the new video is up yet?"

Daniel's videographer had left an hour ago swearing he'd do a quick edit and have it up and running by evening.

Daniel smiled at her. "Could be," he took out his phone and checked the internet, chuckling after a few minutes. He handed her the phone, and she saw a mini Blue Heaven in full party mode. She grinned back at Daniel, delighted.

"I've got to go," Jane said, setting her half full glass of wine down.

Eva handed Daniel his phone.

"We'll look at it later downstairs," she said, partly to piss Marcus off with the hinted-at intimacy, partly because it's what she really wanted to say.

Just as Jane rose to leave, the final party guests came up to say good-bye.

After all the goodbyes were said, just the three of them remained. Awkward. Eva worried Marcus would never leave. "I'd like to talk to you alone, Eva, if I could," he said. Eva reflexively grabbed Daniel's hand and squeezed it hard, her message, she hoped, clear.

"Eva and I have dinner reservations," Daniel said.

They didn't, but Marcus didn't need to know that.

"Oh, well then, maybe I can steal her away for a

minute," Marcus persisted.

Eva gave up, let go of Daniel's hand.

"I'll walk you to your car," she said. But once out the door, she stopped under the shelter of the eaves. It was still raining softly and she didn't want to get wet again.

"I was hoping you'd let me use a cottage for the night. Long drive back to the city and all," Marcus said.

"I'm sorry, Marcus. I'm opening for business in two days and tomorrow morning, very early, the cleaners will be doing the cottages. There are plenty of hotels in Port Huron."

"I really am happy for you, Peanut. I hope you know that."

She nodded. She didn't believe him, couldn't understand why he wouldn't just leave, why he'd even come in the first place.

"I was going to ask you to come to New York with me, but I see that you're settled in here quite nicely."

It was an old trick. He'd used it often to get her to do whatever he'd wanted. Once she'd made an independent decision, he offered a superior alternative, not really offering it but saying, for example, if she was going out for beers with friends, that he had two tickets to see her favorite singer with backstage passes, but he'd find someone else to go with him. He never gave her the opportunity to accept his late offers, and she didn't do so now. She realized with relief that she didn't even want to this time.

"I would have said no," she told him.

He pretended not to hear her.

"So this is really goodbye. And good luck." He bent down to kiss her, but she turned her face so that he caught her cheek instead of her lips.

She headed back into the house before he was even in his car.

"Wow," Daniel said when she came back into the house. "So that's the famous Marcus."

As the din from Marcus's engine faded, they heard shouting coming from Lily's cottage.

Eva noticed a sleek black car pulled off to the side of road. She and Daniel walked over to Lily's cottage and knocked on the door.

"No, Mom! I'm not going, and you can't make me," they heard Lily say. By now Bob was out of his cottage too, and the few of his friends who still hung around were gathered at the door, saying goodbye, slowly heading off.

"Listen, if Lily's mother is really in there, I think you two should go on home and let me handle it."

"Are you sure?" Daniel asked.

When she nodded, they reluctantly left.

Eva had no idea what to do or say now that she was about to be confronted with Lily's mother. What if the woman was a tyrant? What if she tried to take Lily against her will? What would Eva do? Maybe she shouldn't have let Daniel go. At the same time, she knew this was her fight, not his.

As she knocked on the door, Eva's heart skittered. She peered through the open screen. A feeble rain spit on her dry clothes, so she opened the door and entered Lily's cottage.

"Oh hi, Eva. Were we being loud? This is my mother, Mrs. Van Slyke. She's trying to trap me into going home and I'm just not gonna do it. Period."

"Hello, Mrs. Van Slyke, I'm Eva Delacroix, I own

these cottages, and Lily works for me. She's an amazing girl."

For the first time, Mrs. Van Slyke spoke.

"You got the girl part right. My daughter is only seventeen."

Eva's heart skipped a beat.

"She won't be eighteen for another month, and furthermore, when I got here I saw her in a cottage with several young men. They were all drinking. You condone this?"

Eva swallowed, not knowing what to say. She'd meant to have Daniel check on the kids, but had forgotten all about it. Some parent she'd make. She looked at Lily.

"I told her I was eighteen, Ma." Then to Eva, "Sorry. Fake ID. Everybody has them."

"I'm Karen Van Slyke." Lily's mother held out her hand, surprising Eva. "You must be Eva."

Eva took Mrs. Van Slyke's hand, not without trepidation.

"Working as a maid, Lily? Will wonders never cease?" Mrs. Van Slyke's brow was a deep indentation between her eyes.

Lily giggled, a foreign sound that echoed in the empty room. "I didn't do much in Port Austin," she said to Eva.

"Why don't we sit. I'll make coffee." Eve went into the tiny kitchen and busied herself with the chore. Anything to bide time and try to get her pounding heart back to normal. This could ruin her business if Karen Van Slyke decided to press charges.

While Eva made coffee, Lily told her mother about the kittens.

"Eva let me name them!" Lily exclaimed. "There's a mostly black one and a mostly white one, so they're Salt and Pepa. Then there's Nutmeg, she's kind of crazy…"

The whir of the coffee grinder ate the rest of Lily's sentence. Eva opened the tiny fridge, putting cream and sugar on the table, trying not to panic. If Lily's mother talked her into going home two days before her Grand Opening, well, she just couldn't. Eva hadn't realized how indispensable Lily had made herself around here.

Only when the coffee had been poured and they were seated around the table stirring sugar did Lily's mother get to the point of her visit.

"Your therapist tells me you've kept in touch. She showed me the video of this place." Lily's mother said. "Your next appointment was today, and you missed it again, so I came down to take you home."

So, Lily was in therapy. Probably a good thing, seeing as how she was clearly troubled, had outbursts of anger, and was secretive beyond belief. Of course, Eva had chalked all that up to normal teenaged behavior. She'd been wrong about that.

"Has Daddy or Gary agreed to go to a session?" Lily asked.

Eva had no idea what they were talking about until Lily said, "My cousin raped me, and my Daddy doesn't believe it, because my cousin is denying it happened. Or is he sticking to the 'she said yes' story?"

Eva was shocked speechless. Poor Lily. So that is what she'd been dealing with all on her own. Eva could not blame her for running away. Or pretending to be older than she really was.

"No, sweetheart. I'm sorry." Karen took Lily's

hand, but turned to Eva. "I understand you've insured Lily. Her father and I are very grateful, although it was completely unnecessary."

Eva nodded. She felt stunned, tired, and uncertain.

"She's already been accepted at Western this fall," Karen said to Eva. "How can she go to college and be a maid for you?"

Karen's posture was very straight. Her hair was flawless, her jewelry tasteful, her jacket perfectly tailored. Eva, in her jeans and T-shirt, free of make up and hair frizzed from rain, felt a fright sitting next to her. She sipped her coffee.

Lily sat quietly, not saying a word.

"Honey," Eva said to Lily, placing her coffee cup carefully into the saucer. "Of course you should go to college. I always wished I had gone." If Lily was at college, she wouldn't be in danger from any pervert cousin, either.

Karen drained her cup of coffee.

"Would you like another?" Eva asked.

Karen shook her head. "No, thank you." She let the spoon rest inside the empty cup. "I did some checking on you. This place. It's nice."

Eva had a weird feeling, like a combination of pride and resentment. She had no idea what to say.

Lily looked from her mom to Eve.

"You two look alike."

Eva and Karen looked mutually appalled.

"Psych." When Lily laughed, Eva realized how seldom she'd heard her do so.

"Your nails are nice," Karen said, smoothing Lily's hand into her own.

"I could use a coat of clear."

Karen held out her hand for the bottle Lily pulled from her night table drawer. Eva sensed an old ritual. She was happy for Lily. She deserved the kind of bright future a college degree could bring, and it was clear that her mother was going to support her in therapy. Still, the whole thing was just sad.

After her mother had painted Lily's nails, she looked around the cottage.

"It's cute, but I don't see anything of yours here."

"I came with the clothes on my back. And my MP3." Lily didn't say anything to her mom about the room ready for her in the bungalow.

"Well, it's time to go, dear."

Lily nodded.

Eva had known from the minute she'd met Karen. It was for the best.

"I have to say goodbye to Bob," Lily said, dashing out the door before Eva could tell her he had already gone.

Chapter Twenty-Five

Once Eva and Karen were alone, Eva asked a question.

Just as surprisingly, Karen said yes.

Eva went into the house. It was tough going into Lily's room, gathering her things, most of which had been moved in here. Eva used her own suitcase, a pink and purple striped wheelie that had seen better days. She looked around the room, gathering up the tiny supply of trinkets Lily had accumulated while she'd been here. A paperback novel, a bottle of hand lotion, a bag of make up, a hairbrush with blonde strands still in its bristles.

She zipped the bag and came outside wheeling it with one hand, and cradling Ginger, Lily's favorite kitten, in the other.

When Lily saw Ginger in Eva's arms, she started to cry.

"You're keeping it, child," Karen said, putting the suitcase in the trunk while Lily cooed at Ginger.

"It would have been so mean if you brought her out here to make me feel bad for ditching you just before opening," Lily said to Eva.

"You're not ditching me," Eva said. She didn't want to think about the work she'd have to do alone tomorrow. Or how Mama would feel when she discovered one of her kittens gone.

"At least she's old enough," Eva said.

Then she tucked a check into Lily's jeans pocket.

"Your last week's salary and the money for the rights to your film for Bryman House," she said.

"Thanks," Lily said. "I'll add it to the college fund."

It was really over. Lily was getting into the car, Ginger snuggled on her shoulder.

"Tell Bob I said bye. Tell him I'll text!"

As darkness softly fell around her, the rain stopped. Eva watched the taillights of the Cadillac recede down the highway. Lily was gone. Her place, finally ready after weeks of furious activity, was again her own.

The quiet of the cottages without rowdy teenagers, without busy crew people in and out all hours, unsettled her. She shook it off, breathed in the calm scent of a clean earth, of a lake replenished. Lily was with her mother, where she belonged. Bob was back with Daniel. All was in place. With their help, she had realized a dream, done that thing that had seemed so impossible just two short months ago.

Her spirits lifted. She'd accomplished so much.

As she turned to the bungalow, she heard a car on the highway. She kept walking toward her haven even as her ears picked up the sound of tires on gravel. The car had left the highway and turned into her driveway.

Daniel. She knew it was him before she flicked on the porch light and turned to see his black Lexus in the driveway. She stood outside her door, waiting for him.

"Hi." He smiled at her, but his face held concern.

He'd come back. He had known somehow, after all the strength she'd shown in going slow, that tonight she'd feel naked and needy? That, after Marcus, and

Lily, she felt stripped somehow, right down to her lonely, yearning soul?

"I worried maybe Marcus had come back. Just wanted to check that everything was okay here." Daniel reached out a hand and laid it on her arm, just above her elbow. She felt the warmth of his touch right through the sleeve of her shirt.

"No, he didn't." She shook her head, trying to shake off her vulnerability, too.

"Are you okay?"

She was fine about Marcus. Seeing him today had made her realize that, at least. She was over him, without regret.

"It was harder than I thought to let Lily go," she admitted.

"What was her mother like?"

"Fine. They're close. Lily is where she needs to be."

Eva shivered when Daniel dropped his hand from her arm.

"Well, if you're sure, then." His words said goodbye, but his body stood still, the two of them encased in the glow of the porch light.

"Want to come in?" She opened the screen door.

"Sure," he said, his body relaxing into a comfortable ease, making her realize he'd been worried for her. Not the project. Not the Bryman legacy. Her. This was personal. Daniel cared about her.

As they went through to the living room, she snagged a bottle of cognac someone had brought to the party. She didn't have any fancy crystal snifters, so the clear plastic glasses she'd used for the punch would have to do.

"This is nice," Daniel said, toasting her with his drink. "Just us."

"No teenagers," she said, the taste of the liquor, heavy as honey, strong on her tongue.

"No pizza."

"No blaring television."

"We sound like old people," Daniel said, then laughed.

Her heart twisted. To grow old with Daniel. The idea was as sweet, deep, and mysterious as this cognac in her system. And, like the liquor, it went right to her head, making her almost dizzy with longing.

Daniel had made it clear he was finished raising his family. For as much as she'd wanted it, she hadn't even begun. And yet, here they were.

She looked at him. His eyes searched hers. She couldn't think straight. Her mind tumbled out random firings, the way his shirt held the smell of the rain, the way he smiled at her as he reached out to pull her close, the feel of the denim of his shirt as she put her arms around his waist. Her last thought before he kissed her was that he wanted her. Maybe it was only in that simple, uncomplicated way that men wanted women. But right now, she wanted that, too.

His kisses fell like sweet drops of rain on her cheeks, her neck, her lips. They looked at each other; she saw desire in his eyes. Could he see the same in hers? She unbuttoned his shirt as he nibbled her earlobe, letting his teeth drag lightly down her throat, his tongue hot on her neck, then in her mouth. This was the warm center of everything, right here in his arms. She felt safe and cherished and desired. It made her bold and she broke a long kiss to take his hand and lead him into her bedroom.

He walked next to her, moving her shirt up, brushing greedy fingers over the silk of her bra. When they got into her room, she pulled the shirt over her head. Their hands and bodies moved , tearing clothes off, zippers, shoes, every defense down.

Nothing more to hide, they lay skin to skin on the soft quilt of her bed. She felt adored as he tasted every inch of her skin, pulling her nipples into his mouth, igniting new pleasure deep down inside her with each flick of his tongue. Then his fingers found the center of her pleasure and waves of sensation roared over her. She could feel his hardness against her thigh and reached for him, rubbing his silky thickness. He groaned, pushing her hand gently away as he lowered his mouth to taste her. He treated her like a banquet, and took his slow sweet time. She lay across her pillows, open to him completely. She let herself be caressed and cared for, let her mind go while she reveled in the warm sensation of his tongue on her.

His mouth made its lazy way to her belly and she gazed through almost closed lids to see him reach for the condom on her bedside table. Without regret, she took the packet from him, opened it, and slid it down him.

He filled her, his eyes half-closed but still seeing right down into her soul. As he moved, she caught his rhythm. He let her into his heart through his eyes as surely as she'd let him into her body. The feeling was unlike anything she'd ever experienced, as if a ray of light pooled through them, brightening their bodies and bonding them in a mystery she could feel but not understand. It wasn't important to understand with words. The feeling was enough. They moved as one, and they alone filled the world.

She quickened their pace, her heart beating in frantic need. He stayed with her, opening his eyes to gaze down at her, deliberately moving to please her, waiting until he saw the release in her eyes as they drifted completely shut, heard it in the low moan from her throat, felt it in her delicious shudders.

Only when her body's deep throbbing subsided did he stop his slowed movements to rush into her with a final dynamic thrust. Now, he too moaned and lowered his head to the pillow next to hers, their bodies still entwined. He kissed her cheek and as she turned to reach his lips, she opened her eyes again. His were closed, blond lashes against flushed cheeks. She closed her eyes too as they kissed for a long moment, sightlessly devoted.

"I love you," he said.

Her eyelids raised a slit. He was looking right into her, intent, serious.

"I love you, too," was all she could think to reply. It was the truth, and for now, it was more than enough. He pulled her next to him, his arms around her, his body spooning hers. He kissed her back, each tiny bone of her upper spine, then pressed his nose deep into her neck and rested there.

Chapter Twenty-Six

She woke up later, as he covered her with her quilt. Opened her eyes. The light outside her window showed dawn breaking. Before long, the sun would be coming up over the lake. He was already dressed.

"You wouldn't have gone without saying good-bye." It wasn't a question. He'd made her sure of a few things last night. She drew an arm from under the quilt and took his hand in hers. He sat next to her.

"I don't want to leave," he said. "But I know the kind of day you have ahead of you."

"And it's Bob's first day home. He'll wonder where you are."

"He won't be up for hours yet," Daniel said.

As he unzipped his jeans, she moved over to let him slip into bed beside her. This was a new Daniel. The real Daniel. Vulnerable and giving. Kind and gentle. Sweet and protective of those he loved. Including her.

****

Eva had cleaning to do. She thought about calling Wanda, Luke's mom, who had seemed so in charge and at home in her kitchen yesterday. Most of the people in town welcomed paid work, but no, she decided, this was her project and she'd complete the job herself. After a pot of strong coffee, she gathered her cleaning materials and hit the cottages. Lily's first. She tossed every single thing Lily left away. Wrapped the paper ring around the toilet to show it was scrubbed. Folded a point on the bathroom tissue and stuck it with a foil seal. Shined the faucets and filled the mini-fridge with bottled water. She set out the individual coffee packets she'd bought at Costco and the mini-creamers that didn't need refrigeration. She filled an antique sugar bowl.

She changed the sheets and made the bed with hospital corners. She dusted and vacuumed and mopped. And then she did it all again, five more times. It took her twelve hours to get every cottage ready for the guests, and even then, she wanted to do the windows before it got dark. All forty of them, if you included the bungalow.

By ten that night, the bungalow, including the airplane addition, had been polished, waxed, and shined to a high gloss. A high table on the wall of her office held a basket of individually wrapped muffins she'd baked herself as she'd wolfed down take-out pizza. Next to the muffins sat a large wooden bowl of fresh fruit.

Everything was done. She'd cleaned her own bathroom too today, and she couldn't wait to get into a nice warm bubble bath. She turned off her phone. She'd already spoken to Daniel, Jane, and her mother on quick mini-breaks from cleaning. Daniel said he loved her again before they ended their conversation. She told him she loved him back. Everyone wished her luck. Luck, she thought, sinking up to her neck into the lavender scented bath, was just hard work meeting opportunity.

****

The next morning she rose before dawn, refreshed and ready to greet the first day of the rest of her life. This was her favorite part of the day, although she didn't always get to see it. She sat on her porch with a mug of tea and looked out over the water at the rose pink sky splashing across its silver surface.

She thought of her father, because his ashes were scattered there, and because watching the sun rise was a holy experience. She hoped he was in a place where he knew what she'd done, how she was honoring his past. She thought of all of her ancestors, growing up here, every generation, even her own, until the family had scattered. This had once been a working vacation rental property. Now it would be again.

Check in was at eleven, but with the way the sun was shining in the cloudless blue sky, she thought everybody would get here early to make a day at the beach.

By noon she knew she was wrong. Still no arrivals, although she'd been stationed behind her computer for two hours, catching up on email and watching the video of the open house again and again.

She made herself a sandwich and mentally shrugged. Okay, so nobody was here. People got late starts. They would get here when they got here. She had a little thing where people could check off if they were arriving late, but after double and triple checking, she saw that nobody had taken that option. So supposedly, everyone should be here before six. Too late to take advantage of a day at the beach, but still. She'd have a full occupancy to wake up to in the morning. And she was glad about that, because she was getting sort of bored. And nervous.

At three in the afternoon, the phone rang, the first voice she'd heard since the pizza delivery guy last night. She lunged for it.

"Is this Blue Heaven?"

"Yes, this is Eva Delacroix. How may I help you?"

"Well, this is Linda Spellman, we had a reservation you cancelled, but decided to take you up on the offer to come up to Sugar Bush instead. We just wanted to say thank you. This place is amazing."

Eva could not get the words Linda Spellman was saying to make sense.

"I have your reservation right here," she stalled.

"Next week? Right? Luckily, my husband was able to get two weeks off work. So thanks again." And Linda Spellman hung up.

Eva's confusion turned to anxiety. *What the hell?*

She called the other guests who had not arrived, and piece by piece, a pattern began to emerge. All of them had received calls from a woman claiming to be Eva. All of them had been told the cottages wouldn't be ready until next week, but they could come then and also enjoy this week on her at the Sugarbush resort in Traverse City.

Eva didn't argue with what she was told. She tried to sound cheery and in control. The customer, of course, was always right. But something here had gone very wrong. Maybe an internet prank? Could a hacker have gone into her website and messed with her life? Why would someone do that?

Looks like she'd have all week to figure it out. She wanted to call Daniel, but first, opened her bank account. Empty. There was, in fact, a debit mark next to the amount. She kept clicking, looking in her saving account, which was also empty, checking her Visa card balances, way too high to help her now. She'd had several thousand dollars in her checking account yesterday. Now she was minus over a thousand and the loan payment was due in one week. The date she would have run her customer's credit cards and been comfortably solvent.

This was a nightmare.

Every single checking account withdrawal had been credited to Sugarbush Resort.

This went beyond hacking. Someone was out to sabotage her. Marcus? Is that why he'd come up? To get a look at her computer and her passwords? But why? He'd been the one who'd dumped her. He didn't need revenge.

It was after five, which meant the bank was closed, but she called Jane at home, spilling the whole story. Jane was sympathetic, but didn't think it was Marcus.

"Why? Who else would do such a thing?"

"I don't know, but we can get it straightened out Monday morning when the bank opens."

"Think, Jane. Who would do this?"

"Well, I hate to say."

"Please. Tell me."

"You know Daniel. You know how he is about Bryman. And he does own half the bank. He could add your property, which as you know is the only Bryman property on the lake, on any lake, which makes it that much more covetous in Daniel's eyes…oh shit, I hate to even say this. I like Daniel. But this is why I broke up with him. I saw the way he would trick people into selling him their Bryman homes at rock bottom prices. I felt bad about it, but I brokered the deals. I have to take the offer to the client that the buyer submits. That's just business."

Eva couldn't believe, especially after the night they'd spent together, that Daniel was behind this. Maybe he had been a bit of a hustler when he was younger, but he'd changed. He'd mellowed. And he'd done everything he could to help her. Or, maybe, help himself. No, that was ridiculous. Jane was not seeing clearly. She had a past with Daniel that made her bitter.

"Well, it really doesn't matter who did it. What matters is that I get an extension on my payment. I just spent my emergency fund on really nice vacations for three lucky couples." She didn't even want to think about the double booking next week. If she didn't get this straightened out, she might not be the owner of this property by then. That's how tightly the loan agreement was worded.

"Christ," Jane said. "I'll try."

Eva's heart sank.

"One week. I just need a week."

"Well, Daddy might listen to me, but if it's Daniel that did this, he's going to say no. That's the whole point. He didn't want to give you a loan to begin with."

Eva remembered that.

"He's wanted Blue Heaven for as long as I've known him, which is basically forever."

It couldn't be Daniel. It wouldn't be him. He wouldn't do this to her. Even as little things like the way he worked so tirelessly, for free, occurred to her, she was punching his cell phone number. He didn't pick up. She grabbed her keys and drove to his house, calling Marcus on the way. Because she just couldn't bring herself to believe Daniel would do it.

"How could you?" she said, when Marcus picked up on the first ring.

"What? I just wanted to visit. To wish you well."

"You know damn well what I mean."

"No. I don't. Why don't you enlighten me."

So she told him.

"I didn't do that. Why would I do that?"

"You ruined my career before."

"I gave you your career." He was right.

"But then you took it away."

"That was just business. Listen, Peanut. You saw what happened here. What's still happening. It's not personal. I taught you everything you know."

Damn. She believed him.

"Is it money? Because I can give you a loan."

That's when she was sure he didn't do it. Why would he give her money if he'd wanted to ruin her?

Chapter Twenty-Seven

She tried to call Daniel all the way to his house, but he still wasn't answering his phone. She tried Jane again, too, but her phone went right to voice mail. She called Daniel one last time, just as she pulled up to his house. Why wouldn't he pick up?

Bob answered the door.

"Is Daniel here?"

"Hi there, Eva."

She'd already pushed her way inside.

"What's up?"

"I need to speak to Daniel."

"He's not here." Bob yawned.

"Where is he? When will he be back?" Her eyes cast about the front room. Empty. She almost looked under the sofa, but instead moved into the kitchen. Bob followed.

"Port Huron. I don't know when he'll be back."

Port Huron? "What's he doing there?"

"Hey, Eva, take it easy. Is something wrong?"

"Bob. Why is Daniel in Port Huron and when will he be home? Why isn't he picking up his cell?"

Bob poured a cup of coffee. Took his time stirring in cream and sugar. Eva wanted to shake him. "He went to a sports bar with the guys. They were getting rooms in PH. Nobody wanted to drive back home after."

So, maybe he couldn't hear his cell phone over the

music. Or maybe he'd turned it off. She tried to keep her panic at bay.

"He's coming back tomorrow?"

"He said he'd be home to make breakfast, so yeah," Bob said.

She had a good mind to drive to Port Huron right now and go through every sports bar in the town looking for him. Then she checked the clock. It was after eleven. She'd get to PH by midnight or a little after. And then how many bars would she have to troll before she found the one he was in? What if it wasn't a sports bar? What if it was a strip joint? Did Port Huron even have topless dancing? Her mind was a cesspool and she felt so low she couldn't even think right.

On the drive home, Jane called. Her voice full of regret, she said her dad had decided to call in the loan if it wasn't paid by next Friday.

"I'm sorry, honey. I'll work on him some more."

Eva could barely thank her friend. She didn't want to talk anymore. She had a weird hopeless hope that Daniel could explain everything. Maybe it had something to do with the magazine. Maybe he'd wanted to have the place empty for the photographer and the writer. But why would he use her money? And not talk to her about it first? She wished she had a pill she could take to make it all go away but the best she could come up with out of her medicine cabinet was Tylenol PM.

****

Eva woke groggy from the Tylenol, a tinny taste in her mouth. She'd remembered waking feeling like this, utterly helpless and lost, many times. But not recently. She brushed her teeth for five minutes. It didn't help; her mouth still tasted bad. Her heart still hurt. This time it was so much worse. Last time, she'd lost her boyfriend and her job and the economy tanked. This time, she'd lost her family's legacy. How would she tell her mother?

She checked her cell but Daniel still had not called. That made him seem guiltier than ever, and yet, she still held out hope that there was some explanation. He'd said he loved her. She couldn't quite believe he'd do this to her. And all the folks she'd talked to said a woman called them. Not that Daniel didn't have access to women. Of course he did. She cursed the little corner of her heart that refused to believe that Daniel had betrayed her.

Eva called the lawyer she'd used to handle all her other business. He wasn't picking up his phone, since it was Saturday, but she left him a message.

Then she threw on the jeans she'd worn yesterday and drove over to Daniel's house. If the bastard wouldn't answer his phone, she'd just wait there for him. It's not like she was needed at home.

"Bob answered the door in only his boxers, rubbing sleep from his eyes. "He's still not here."

"Well, I'm coming in and waiting for him."

"Suit yourself." Bob shrugged, went upstairs and came back down with clothes on.

"You can quit calling him," Bob said, making coffee in the kitchen. Coffee. Eva had forgotten about ordinary things like caffeine this morning. The smell of the fresh roasted beans drew her into the kitchen with Bob.

"I keep thinking he'll pick up."

"But he won't. I found his cell in his room, on the floor. There's like, sixty calls from you. It must have fallen out of his pocket when he got dressed to go to PH with the guys. You want to tell me what this about?"

Eva told him.

Bob whistled.

"Daniel wouldn't do that."

"I don't want to think so, but I can't think of anyone else who would."

"Me either," Bob said. "It sounds crazy. But don't worry. We're loaded. Daniel will loan you the money to pay your bills, and then your customers will come next week, and you'll be fine."

Eva's phone rang then, and she hoped it might be Daniel, but she didn't recognize the number. She answered, talked for a few minutes, and then hung up.

"That was the guy from the magazine. Arriving on schedule with his photographer. He has a hotel booked in Port Huron. He gave me the number." That quashed her last threadbare theory about Daniel wanting his friend to stay on the premises and maybe wanting a vacant property to photograph. It hadn't made sense at the time, but she so wanted to believe this was just a big mix up, another one of Daniel's plans to make things better for her, if only she'd do things his way.

"See. I told you it wasn't Daniel. Why would he ruin the one thing he's wanted more than anything? He's been after that guy forever to do a piece on Blue Lake."

Eva allowed another tiny sliver of hope to wedge itself into her hurting heart. But then, a little voice whispered that Daniel could still get the press. The article would still be published. Except now Blue Heaven would be his.

She and Bob drank coffee. They ate Cheerios.

When the hour got sufficiently proper to make a call, in Bob's estimation, he called the hotel in Port Huron where Daniel said he was staying. Daniel had checked out.

"See, he'll be home in an hour and we'll get this entire thing straightened out."

Eva kept wondering what to tell her mother. Or when to give up on Daniel and call the police. She would not ask her mom, her sweet retired schoolteacher mom living on a fixed income, to dip into her life savings to bail out her loser daughter.

"What did you tell the guy from the magazine?"

"I acted like everything was fine."

"So they're coming."

"Yep."

"Lily really wanted to meet them. Especially the photographer."

Eva noticed for the first time that Bob didn't seem much happier than she was, and she knew it wasn't her situation. It was Lily, of course. He missed her.

"Have you heard from Lily?"

"Nope. You?" Bob's voice lifted in hope.

"No. But then I didn't expect to."

"You don't think Lily would have…" Bob hesitated, then said "No."

"No." Eva agreed.

"She'd have no reason," Bob said. "I mean, I love Lily, so I think she's perfect and would never do anything wrong, but also, she doesn't have a motive. In the television shows, you always need a motive."

"The problem is, there's nobody with a motive. Except Daniel."

"But Daniel wouldn't do it," Bob insisted.

"I hope you're right."

"I am. And you're making me mad talking about him like that, after everything he's done for you. He loves you the way I love Lily. Don't you know that? Why are women so stupid?"

Bob stormed out of the room, leaving Eva to ponder the idea that Daniel loved her. He'd told her so. Twice. Right before he disappeared at the exact same time as all her money. Bob returned a few minutes later, sheepishly hanging his head.

"Sorry," he said.

"It's okay. Why don't you call Lily? Not about what happened to me. Just to talk. I'm going to go over to Jane's and see if she can ask her dad again for an extension on my loan. And then I think I better drive out to the Sheriff's in Delton."

****

Eva turned onto Jane's block and saw Daniel's car in the driveway. Her stomach flipped, so she pulled over before she reached Jane's.

She got out of her car and walked toward Jane's house, cutting across the lawn to the front door. In the picture window, she saw Jane and Daniel, champagne glasses in hand, toasting.

Toasting. The scene took a minute to make sense, but only a minute. They were toasting the fact that they'd wrested Blue Heaven from her. They only had eyes for each other and neither noticed as she turned away and walked back to her car.

Chapter Twenty-Eight

From the first, a part of her had known he would betray her. Intellectually, intuitively, she'd known there was still something there between Jane and Daniel. But her emotions, her neediness, made her blind to the truth.

All the signs had been there, she just hadn't wanted to see them.

Exactly like Mom always said, she was relearning her lesson, all over again.

Both Marcus and Daniel had money and power. Both wanted something from her. Sex, but also something else. Marcus had wanted her youthful take on advertising. Daniel had wanted Blue Heaven. And she'd believed both of them when they told her they loved her.

The worst part was that with Daniel, she thought she'd done everything right. She thought she'd been cautious. She thought she'd matured, learned wisdom. But no, dumb as ever.

No wonder he didn't mind working long hours for her. No wonder he hired extra crew at his own expense, paid more for materials than her budget allowed. He knew the place would eventually be his.

Even at the bank, he'd stepped down as an active employee so there'd be no conflict of interest. Hell, he probably put his share of the bank in Bob's name just to make everything nice and legal. So many signs and she'd missed them all.

As she drove toward Delton, Eva thought more about how it would be to live in a town where she'd been made a complete fool of by two of its leading citizens. And further, the court battle she was bound to be headed into. She saw no way out. And she had no money to pay lawyers, while Daniel and Jane had bucks to burn. She was nobody and they were everybody who'd ever hurt her. She should just leave town. Sarasota was supposed to be a really nice place. Her mom said they had a great downtown with art galleries and coffee shops.

Her heart burned with grief. To leave all she'd worked for. To admit defeat. Blue Lake didn't have a police department. The county had a Sheriff's office two towns down and that's the way she pointed her car.

The Sheriff's office in Delton was a squat brick building. There were only two cars in the large asphalt lot, so she parked as far away as possible from the six or seven orange suited jailbirds behind a tall fence topped with barbed wire who were presumably out for fresh air and exercise.

She wasn't afraid of the criminals. She just didn't want to look at them. Same way she had not wanted to look at the truth about Jane and Daniel.

She shouldered her handbag and walked into the glass front door. At another set of glass doors, she saw a bored looking dispatch operator, a woman. Her voice boomed over a speaker "Can I help you?"

"I need to speak to the Sheriff. Someone hacked into my bank account and stole all my money."

"Deputy Montclare is in."

The woman buzzed the doors and they opened.

"Purse." It took Eva a second to realize her purse would be searched. As the woman pawed through her wallet and gum and sunglass case, Eva studied her outfit. A tan uniform of shirt and pants that reminded her of the park ranger in Yogi Bear cartoons.

The dispatcher handed her purse back. "Name?"

"Eva Delacroix."

"What's the problem?"

Eva explained.

"You're in luck. Montclare is out resident computer gee—expert."

She picked up her phone and spoke into it. Eva could see two hallways, one presumably led to the jail, the other to offices. Dispatch Woman pointed down the hall on the left. Eva started to walk that way when a guy appeared dressed just like the woman she'd left at her desk, except for a shiny badge on his pocket and a gun at his side.

"Come right in, Ms. Delacroix." Deputy Montclare was young, but he listened intently as she told her story, which was also being recorded by a tiny device on the desk between them.

He pushed the recorder off and got up. "I'll just make a few calls and then we will head over to your place to collect evidence and dust for prints."

"But I know who did it! I told you!"

"I understand. We're just verifying. Proof. Right?"

"Okay," she said as his desk phone rang.

He picked up the phone. Spoke into it, his eyes shooting to lock with hers and then break contact. Not once, not twice, three times. What was going on?

Eva tuned into the one-sided conversation.

Deputy Montclare said, "She's injured? Where?

How critical?"

"Good thing you came here," Deputy Montclare said, walking her out to her car. "You have the tightest alibi in the world."

"Was it Jane? Is she hurt?" This was unreal. Could she really not know Daniel at all? Had he hurt Jane?

"Non-fatal. If your story pans out, she'll go to trial. Your office is a crime scene. Don't go back there until I phone you."

Deputy Montclare left her to her broken heart and burning questions. Not somebody, but something had died. Inside of her. She drove home. She didn't stop at Daniel's or Jane's or the antique store. She didn't stop in Eddie's for a burger. It was a gorgeous sunny day. If she had customers, they'd be at the beach. Maybe not swimming, but taking in the sunshine after a long Michigan winter.

The cops were at her place, crime scene tape blocking the office entrance. She went in the lake side door, and lay on her bed. Mama and kittens covered her with licks and purrs. It felt lovely, but her brain wouldn't turn off, no matter how much she wanted it to. Even this room, her first sanctuary when she'd moved to Blue Lake, now had uncomfortable associations.

Daniel had made love to her here. That was one part of the equation that just didn't add up, something she had not told the deputy. Why did he have to seduce her? To say he loved her and wanted to try to have a real relationship with her? Sure, guys liked to score, and some of them lied to do so, but it didn't make sense. How could Jane say yes to that part of the plan? And when had Daniel become such a convincing actor?

She sat on the bed, disrupting Mama and the

kittens, who all began grooming themselves as if nothing were amiss. What she needed to do, if for no other reason than her foolish pride, was to confront Daniel. She had to know, had he been the one to hurt Jane? She quaked at the idea.

She put on some makeup and did her hair. Daniel would regret messing with Eva Delacroix.

Chapter Twenty-Nine

After Bob told Daniel what had transpired that morning, he didn't stop to charge his phone. Eva was at the sheriff's anyway filing a report. Instead he went straight to Jane's to confront her. It would take two minutes and then he'd call Eva.

He wished he had not gone to Port Huron last night. But it was fine. Or would be. He could fix this. He'd do anything for Eva. After he was finished with Jane, she would pay. She'd committed bank fraud. That had to be at least a felony.

He pulled his car into Jane's driveway, got out and slammed the door hard. He felt like he had too much angry energy. He had to be careful not to do anything stupid but to calmly tell Jane that this was the end of her life as she knew it.

Jane answered the door wearing tight workout shorts and a crop top. Her hair was piled on top of her head but she clearly had not broken a sweat. She'd been waiting for him. What he had hardly wanted to believe was suddenly clear. All the signs were there in her crazy eyes. This had happened, but not on such a grand scale, before.

"I've been waiting for you." Jane held her door open until Daniel went into her house. He got the chills just being in the same room with her. She must have stopped taking her meds a while ago if she'd gone this far.

Before Daniel could process a word, Jane grabbed him and kissed him hard on the lips. Disgusted, he pulled away. She hadn't tried anything like that in over a year. He'd been sure she was finally over him, over her delusions that they'd get back together again. When they were younger, that was the pattern, but not for years now.

Daniel remembered how she'd had him in thrall after his folks died. She'd convince him to skip school, bring over porn, weed, and apple wine. They'd have sex for entire afternoons while Bob was in school, only leaving the bed to grab some food. He hadn't always been the perfect parent, but eventually, the sharp shock of his parents' deaths dulled, and he pulled himself together. He got rid of Jane. Or so he thought.

He noticed the champagne chilled and waiting in crystal glasses. She'd obviously had done some sipping before he'd arrived, but it was like she knew he'd be coming. After he broke off the kiss, she twirled away like a little girl in a party dress, grabbed the champagne, handed him a glass.

"We did it!" She held her glass high in the air before clicking it with his. Daniel, stunned by the kiss and everything Bob had told him, stunned that this was a woman who had committed a major crime, a federal offense, and she wanted to celebrate with him. He set the glass of champagne on a side table without touching a sip.

"I had nothing to do with whatever you did, Jane. How could you steal Eva's money?"

"You can't prove I did that. Nobody can."

Daniel thought about Port Huron. His friend who'd

taped the video the afternoon of the open house had been with the group. He'd told Daniel there was some strange footage of Jane. "He got you on tape. At the open house. When you used Eva's computer? He filmed it."

That shut her up. For a second.

"But I did it for you." Jane drank off her glass of champagne and threw the empty glass onto her brick hearth. It shattered. She went over to the glass and deliberately chose a piece, quickly slashing across her wrist with the sharp end. Blood started flowing. Daniel knew then she was out of her mind. She was high or drunk or having another breakdown; it was hard to tell.

"Now we have the resort." She started coming at him with the bloody piece of sharp glass.

"Jane drop the glass. Give me your arm. You're hurt. We have to stop the bleeding."

Jane did exactly as he asked.

He speed-dialed Jane's father and put his phone on speaker so Augustine could hear what was happening while Daniel tried to wrap the wound.

"Call 911," Daniel said as soon as Paul said hello. And then to Jane, "Why did you cut yourself? You're bleeding. Let me wrap your arm up. We need to get you to the doctor." He wanted Paul to hear that.

Jane seemed dazed as Daniel pulled her into the kitchen and used snowy white towels to staunch the blood on her arm, and to buy time.

"Your dad is calling an ambulance." Daniel only hoped it was true. "And you've got to return the money you stole from Eva's account." Jane seemed impervious to the pain those wounds would certainly cause.

"Honey, we can give her back the funds after we

foreclose," Jane said, bleeding and drunk but still making deals. 'We'll pick up the property at a good price, I can negotiate the hell out of that one. She's got to see, with you and me and my dad, who's going to believe her against the three of us? Not to mention, she has like zero money for a lawyer."

Daniel hoped old man Augustine had called 911. And that he was still listening.

"But what you did was illegal, Jane."

"Nobody has to know."

Daniel had never wished himself somewhere else as hard as he did right now. Somewhere nice with Eva, walking on the beach, sitting in her bungalow on a rainy night. He had taken Eva for granted. He realized now how much he loved her and needed her in his life. Meanwhile, Jane had calmed. She seemed to like him holding the towel around her arm and talking things over.

Jane's father came. It seemed like hours later, but it was probably only ten minutes. By then the bleeding had stopped and Daniel knew she hadn't done any serious damage to a vein or artery. He explained what she'd done to Paul, and left him to take care of his daughter.

****

Daniel drove home. He didn't need to call Eva. Her car was on the curb in front of his house. He came into the living room. She sat there with Bob. Eva's eyes were closed, her head thrown back against the sofa.

She opened them when he said her name.

He told her everything that had happened at Jane's.

"This is crazy," she said, not moving a muscle. Just looking at him with a hot intensity. He knew she had to be fatigued. Probably hadn't slept. He wished he could take care of her, but first, they had to get through this horrible thing. Because it still wasn't over.

Eva told him what the deputy had said after formally taking her complaint down and he'd gotten that phone call. He hadn't said anything else. "My office is a crime scene!"

Daniel didn't know the end of the story yet, either. When he'd left, he assumed Paul had taken Jane to the hospital. But there had been some pieces he had been able to put together again. Eva's pieces.

"Before I left, Paul, that's Augustine's name. Jane's father, assured me that the funds will be back in your account before Monday." Daniel pulled Eva into his arms and held her. She didn't resist, simply put her head on his shoulder. "He's going to revise the fine print on your loan, get you a better interest rate and a less cutthroat foreclosure stipulation. Plus you won't have to pay on the loan until September. It is the least he can do for you."

Eva slumped against Daniel with relief. "It's still a mess, but I can work with it. What's going to happen to Jane? Isn't bank fraud a federal offense?"

Daniel held her close. She felt so good. He never wanted to let her go. He didn't want to spend another minute without her. He couldn't imagine them spending the winter apart. "This all happened less than an hour ago, so I'm not sure."

"My God, you poor man," Eva said. Typical of her, even now, she wasn't thinking of herself, but of him. Of course, he was sure she was relieved that her financial situation had been resolved, or was fast on the way to resolution.

"So what was the proof you had? That you told Jane about?"

"This." Daniel clicked on the uncut video footage that his buddy had given him in Port Huron. Certain sections had not appeared on the internet, but they were juicy if you knew the background. He fast-forwarded and zoomed into Jane at Eva's desk, with the time stamp clear. Just before the bank transfer had taken place. Within minutes.

"You can't see what she's doing."

"She didn't know that. And there's enough proof there for any court of law."

"So during the party she went into my files," Eva said. Daniel's heart ached for her. She just didn't know how crazy Jane could get when she went off her meds and started drinking. And really, he hadn't, either. She'd pulled crap before that her father had explained away, but nothing this bad. Jane must have sensed how much he truly loved Eva. "I knew it was stupid to keep all my passwords in my top drawer." Eva rested her head on his shoulder.

"Didn't Jane help you with the art on your website?"

"Yeah, we were at that computer together plenty of times. She knew the way to my site, knew how my bookings are set up. It would be easy for her to locate the contact info of my guests. I feel like an idiot for ever trusting her."

"Try being me. I dated that woman for years."

"I guess you have a point."

Then the bell rang. Through the glass insert on the door, they could make out the faces of Paul and Jane Augustine standing on the porch.

Chapter Thirty

A sheriff's car was outside, parked in front of the house. Daniel pulled out a copy of the video He'd sent a copy via email to the sheriff the minute he'd seen the thing his buddy had alerted him to on the video. At the time, they'd been drinking and neither of them had any idea what it meant.

"I swear I didn't ask them to come," Daniel said.

"No. I know. But I want to see her," Eva said.

Daniel let them in. Eva had never met Paul Augustine, but now he looked to her like a beaten old man. His face sagged with sorrow and his jowls vibrated with emotion.

Eva had never seen Jane so messed up. Her hair was snarled, her wrist was bandaged, she stumbled when she walked. Maybe the doctor had given her a pain pill. She didn't seem like the same person Eva thought she knew.

Daniel sat back down next to Eva on the sofa and Jane plopped gracelessly into a chair opposite them. Paul Augustine stood behind Jane, one hand on her shoulder.

Jane's eyes were shot with red as if every blood vessel in her whites had popped. She looked like she had a major case of pink eye. And her nose was red as well. She looked more defeated than crazy, as if her acts of lunacy in the past few days were a grand experiment that had failed.

"Thank you for seeing us, Eva." Paul Augustine stood behind Jane's chair with his hand on her shoulder. "Jane has something she'd like to say to you."

Jane pulled in a shaky breath. She had not so far met Eva's eyes. She was instead looking down at her bare legs, tanned and toned, below her workout shorts. The irrelevant thought that spooled through Eva's head was that it was too early in the season to be tan. Jane probably went to a spa in Port Huron to spray tan herself. Why hadn't she noticed Jane's self-absorption before? Her vanity? Her insanity?

Eva didn't know why she was focusing on such silly details. It could be that her heart hurt, still. She'd really believed that in Jane she'd found a friend for life. But it had all been a lie.

Jane looked up, looked Eva right in the eye.

"I did like you, you know," she said.

It wasn't exactly an apology. When Daniel had told her what really happened, she'd felt things slot back into perfect place. But no. There was one piece missing here, one thing that would never be right again. Her friendship with Jane. Which had been a lie from the minute Jane had introduced herself in the bar. Paul Augustine's hand squeezed his daughter's shoulder with a bit more pressure.

"I can't, Daddy. I just can't say I'm sorry for trying to win him back."

"You don't have to say that, honey. What you need to apologize for is trying to ruin Ms. Delacroix's business. You need to apologize for accessing her personal accounts and creating havoc in her life."

"I do apologize for that," Jane said, woodenly, but

again looking down and not at Eva. "I don't want to go to jail," she said.

Eva felt torn. Nobody should be offered a get out of jail free card just because they were rich.

"That's not up to me."

Paul Augustine nodded. Jane stared blankly at her manicure. Man-eating red, Eva noticed. To match her eyes. Which was when Eva realized something. Jane might be rich. She might be privileged. But she suffered too. She might even have legitimate mental problems, Eva didn't know about that, but she did know about suffering, and about wanting something, or someone, so bad that you'd do almost anything to make it happen. Hadn't she done that with Blue Heaven? Of course, she'd used legal means. But still. This entire incident would be a minor blip on the screen of her life—if she could believe that Jane would never do anything like this again. She never wanted to see Jane again. She didn't want to live in the same town as her.

"I don't want to live here, seeing the two of them all the time, holding hands. It would make me sick." Jane found a hangnail and tore it off so violently that her finger beaded with blood. She wiped it on her bare leg. Mr. Augustine pretended not to notice.

"There are places for people like my daughter," Paul said to Daniel and Eva, "secure facilities where she will get the help she needs."

Eva realized he was talking about a mental hospital. Probably a really nice one where Jane would be comfortable and sheltered, but also get the help she so obviously needed.

Jane seemed to have no sense of what she'd done wrong. There was no remorse. Maybe she was drugged, or maybe she was a sociopath. Eva didn't know.

"It's not up to us. Jane's fate is out of our hands," Daniel said.

"See," Jane said, looking up again into Eva's eyes. She stuck her bloody finger where the wound had beaded up in her mouth and sucked. Then she took it out, inspected it, smiled, maybe pleased that it was clean. "He still worries about me. He cares about me, and there's not a thing you can do about that. He only loves you because you have the prime Bryman property…"

Jane would have gone on, but her father said "Jane!" in the sternest tone he'd used yet. "Enough!" Paul yanked Jane's arm and she stood. "I think we've said enough for today."

Deputy Montcalm was on the porch. Paul walked Jane to the sheriff's vehicle. He kissed her and then let the deputy drive her away.

"She'll be out on bail by morning." Eva was so tired. She just wanted life to go back to normal.

"They may realize she's a flight risk and deny bail." Daniel hugged her tight and she let him.

****

For the rest of the day that started so badly and ended so well, Daniel took care of Eva. He drove her home to check on the cats. The police tape was gone, so was her laptop. Daniel made her dinner at his place. He gave her a cup of tea and a stack of shelter magazines he'd bought at the bookstore in Port Huron. Then he sat with his laptop, figuring out, he said, the logistics of her second, overbooked week. She just couldn't handle one more detail, so she'd been happy to let him have a go at solving the overbooking problem. She had no idea what he'd say to her customers or how he'd work it out, but he vowed everyone would be satisfied.

Eva felt as if she were being taken care of. She felt safe, and loved. She looked at the photos in the magazines, not bothering to read the articles. It reminded her.

"The magazine photographer and writer will be here Monday."

Daniel looked up from his laptop. In all the Jane craziness, Eva knew he'd forgotten that, too. She could see the wheels turning. Daniel had looked forward to the magazine people seeing a full house, but Blue Heaven would be empty.

"I'm just finishing up," he said. "I don't think it will be a problem. After all, they're doing the piece on the entire town."

She nodded and went back to flipping through *American Bungalow*. After an hour or so, Daniel logged off. She put down her magazine when he got up from the desk and came to sit with her on the couch.

Since she was sitting with her feet stretched across the sofa, he picked them up and put them on his lap, absently giving her a delicious foot rub in the process.

"Here's my idea. Three couples took the Sugarbush week and signed on for next week at Blue Heaven as well. That means nine reservations and six cottages."

Eva nodded.

"So, we move the three couples who are at Sugarbush this week into the bungalow."

"Where will I sleep?" Eva didn't like it, but she had to admit it was a good solution. She'd have never thought of it, because it meant she'd lose privacy and have to sleep on her sofa. Not her idea of a workable solution, but hell, she'd make it work, even if she had to sleep in the gazebo.

"That's my other idea. You sleep here. With me and Bob. Bring Mama and the kittens if that makes you feel better."

She nodded. "You certainly have enough bedrooms."

"I was sort of hoping you'd share my room."

"What about corrupting a minor?"

"Bob knows we're in love."

There was that word. The one that made her heart melt. And it had to be true. He had to love her to go to so much trouble for her. Every action he'd taken today, really almost since the day he'd met her, showed how much he cared.

But things had not really been resolved between them. He was still going to Georgia, and she'd still be here without him. Sure, he'd promised to return, but she didn't want a long-distance relationship. Of course, she was going to take it, like it or not, because the other option, breaking up, was just not acceptable.

"I do love you," she said. "If I didn't know before, today sealed the deal. You're amazing."

"You used to say I was bossy."

"Sometimes it's nice to know your lover's got your back."

"Good, because there's more."

Geez. What else? She was still thinking about strangers taking over her bungalow. That was weird. She couldn't quite get comfortable with the idea. Maybe she'd sleep at Daniel's but remain in the kitchen and living room of her place every day from breakfast until midnight.

"Remember how we talked about getting Luke's mom and her friend to help you clean and take care of things around here?"

She nodded.

"Well, they're starting tomorrow. And next week, one of them will be on the premises at all times, from 6 a.m. until 2 a.m. or whenever the last guest goes to bed."

"I can deal with that." Eva was so grateful she wanted to fling herself into Daniel's arms. But then again, the foot rub felt good, too.

"Your cash flow problems are over, so I offered them the going rate for service help."

"Let me guess. Cash."

He laughed. "No, but I added enough to their base pay to cover taxes. Everybody wins."

"You've thought of everything."

Daniel smiled. "Wanda is going to make coffee and do a continental breakfast for everyone upstairs. There will be fresh cookies for the kids and cocktails for the grownups in the gazebo at six, board games and soft drinks on the porch, and a van to drive anyone who wants transportation into town for a day of shopping, lunch, or dinner and back to Blue Heaven whenever they're ready to return."

Eva sat up, her feet and body totally relaxed from Daniel's ministrations. He'd incorporated every single idea they'd talked about through the weeks. Even the ones that seemed too much to hope for, like a van and extra help.

"You did all that in an hour?"

"Technically, it was two, but who's counting?"

"So, this van, will it be giving tours of the town

that Bryman built?"

"How'd you guess?"

"And I bet Bob's driving."

He nodded. "I'll do the talking, he'll do the driving. At least next week. I plan to hire someone to give the tour after that."

"What about your friend that did the videos? Didn't you say he only works part time?"

Daniel nodded. "We make a great team," he said.

She hugged him and he gave her a long and lingering kiss.

"Thank you," she said. He truly was her Superman.

"Don't mention it," he said, kissing her again.

She felt his kisses down to her toes, made her want to be somewhere horizontal with him, preferably in a place that Bob couldn't pop into at any moment.

"In the interest of testing out your plan, I think I'd like to see your bed now. You know, to try out the mattress, see if I can sleep in it through the night."

"We can do that," Daniel said.

****

Daniel's bedroom made her sad. The furniture was clearly his parents', except for the new king-sized bed. She'd been on that bed before. She remembered what they'd said. She put it out of her mind by stripping naked as quickly as possible and diving onto the inviting bed. She watched him undress, just a bit behind her. He laughed as he joined her naked on the bed. Their bodies entwined, she laughed too. They'd been through hell today and made it all the way to heaven.

They kissed and Daniel moved his hands all over her skin, exploring every inch of her, stopping to take her breasts into his mouth. She moaned and let all the pent up energy of the day take her. She moved one leg and in a smooth rhythm she was on top of him. She lifted herself and guided him inside, then moved herself up and down, rubbing herself against him, making them both wild.

They made love like the lake in a storm, churning, crashing, returning when he watched her come and let himself go. They locked eyes. She could feel him spurting into her. Oh. Her eyes widened. He just smiled. They hadn't used a condom.

Exhaustion finally hit her. She was spent, physically, emotionally, sexually. But Daniel's bed was an oasis of peace. Her head fell into soft pillows.

"That didn't happen on purpose," she said.

"I know." He turned to her and smoothed her hair. "It's fine. It doesn't matter."

She wanted to talk more, but it also felt good just to close her eyes and drift in his embrace.

Chapter Thirty-One

They lingered in bed long after they should have been up and eating the dinner he cooked. She told him about the first day at the bank, how his glasses reminded her of Clark Kent, and how she'd hoped in some tiny corner of her heart that he was there to rescue Blue Heaven. "And you did," she said.

"I'm not Superman," he said. "Just a builder. And, don't forget, Lois Lane, we did it together."

Desire showed in the way he moved his leg to hook it over hers, bringing her closer. It showed in the way he inclined his whole body toward her, and kissed her, and made love to her again. Still no condom.

"Something's different about you," Eva said, after they both woke up from the nap neither meant to take. It was dark outside. The house was quiet. Not even the sound of the lake in the background.

"Maybe it's that I finally found you," Daniel said.

"You're so sweet." But what she was thinking was *You will be in Georgia and I will be here for six months alone and that doesn't seem to bother you at all.*

Eva's mother always said worry about tomorrow, tomorrow and today right now. Right now, she was hungry. They'd been in bed for hours and food had been the furthest thing from their minds. Now it was all she wanted to think about. Nothing beyond the next meal.

****

Eva had resigned herself to a week without Blue Heaven guests when a woman, man, and teenager showed up Monday morning.

"We hear you have cottages to rent," the woman said, a wide smile on her face.

"I do," Eva said. She'd flipped on the vacancy sign out by the highway. Maybe they'd seen it driving by. There was something familiar about the woman, who was shaking her head, still smiling, but Eva couldn't put her finger on it. Then a station wagon pulled in behind the new guests' car and out piled another family. Two younger children and matching parents. Then a third car arrowed in behind them, and a fourth.

The first woman had just finished signing the registration book and handed Eva her card. The last name was not familiar but the first one rang a big bell.

"Marcie?"

"We wondered when you'd figure it out," her cousin Marcie said. They all had big smiles pasted on their faces as her cousins introduced their children. She'd played dolls with Marcie's little sisters, and now here they were with little ones of their own. Marcie's teenager had already gone upstairs.

"Cool," he said, coming back down. "But where's the TV? And I hope you have cable."

These were not ordinary guests. She opened her pocket doors and showed Marcie's son through. Who was he, her second cousin? Or first cousin once removed? She always got that mixed up.

"In here." She pointed out the television in her living room.

"You need to get a Wii for upstairs," he said, clicking the remote and settling in on her couch.

Marcie had followed him into Eva's quarters.

"My God, what you've done with this place!"

"I know. Well, it wasn't me. It was a whole bunch of people."

"But you made it happen."

Eva still couldn't get over the fact that her cousins were all here. "I sent those pamphlets to your last known address, but wasn't sure they'd find you."

"Oh, they did. We saw the video, went to your website, tried to call, but by the time we all got a date together, you were booked. Then your friend Daniel called us and told us that you had unexpected openings, but it had to be now. So we all just said 'we're doin' it.'"

Eva was overwhelmed. It felt good to have people in the house again, but these weren't just people. These folks were her family. Eva took Marcie and the girls through the house, while their husbands checked out the exteriors. She was just about to take them upstairs when Georgie, her only male cousin, went right behind the registration counter and took the cottage keys and handed them around while the guys started unpacking cars. She smiled. That's the way they'd always done it in the past. The fathers handed out the keys. It was a tradition Georgie clearly felt entitled to carry on. Eva didn't mind.

Walking up the stairs, she rejoiced. Just like that, four of her six cottages were rented. All due to Daniel. He was amazing, as her cousins agreed when they saw his work.

"So this Daniel is your builder, your problem-solver, and your boyfriend?"

"Yep."

"Cool."

"When are we gonna meet him?"

"He'll be over later with a couple of guys doing a magazine story on the town."

Which reminded Eva. She needed to make a trip to the grocery store. They'd have a big barbecue dinner. Daniel had already planned to grill steaks for the magazine people. She'd just buy more steaks. And potatoes. And corn.

Before she could tell Marcie she'd be right back, Daniel pulled up with someone sitting next to him. Really? Could it be? Daniel swung open his door and rushed to open the passenger side. Eva's mom appeared, her hand on Daniel's arm. Eva ran to her mom. As they hugged, Eva smiled at Daniel through the tears of happiness in her eyes.

Her mother, once Eva stopped hugging long enough to see her, looked younger than when she'd lived in Michigan. Her hair was pure white, and she was tiny, but she was strong and her cheeks had roses in them.

"Would you look at his place?" Her mother wasn't even looking at the house, but out at the lake, where they'd laid Dad to rest.

Eva hugged Daniel. "Thank you," she said.

"Mom, it's so good to see you." She switched the hug back to her mom.

"Your boyfriend here wouldn't take no for an answer. He bought me a first class ticket, so how could I say no? I've never flown first class in my life!"

Then Marcie and the rest of the family piled out of their cottages and a general reunion ensued. It was just like the old days, everyone talking at once, laughter ringing out, stories tumbling one after the other. Everyone was older now; this was the next generation. She wished her dad was here to see it.

After Eva settled her mother in the room that would have been Lily's, she told Marcie, who was unloading a huge shopping bag of snack foods onto the top of the fridge, that she'd be back in an hour.

Daniel had returned to the airport to pick up the magazine people, and Eva had promised to have the food ready for dinner at six. Marcie's husband and Georgie were carrying an enormous cooler down to the beach. Kids of various ages followed. Eva would never remember all their names.

"Do you need towels?" she asked Marcie.

"Nope. Brought our own."

"It's so good to see you."

"You too. Maybe you can come down to the beach?"

"I wish! Maybe tomorrow. Right now, I'm going to pop over to the store and then I'm going to make potato salad. I want to have a big family dinner, like in the old days."

"I hope the potato salad tastes just like your mom's."

"If I'm lucky, she'll be rested from her nap and make it herself."

"Remember how our mothers never came to the beach? They'd be in the kitchen cooking all day and sitting out watching the water from the front yard in the evening."

"I still do a fair amount of that." Eva adored her new porch, she couldn't wait until Marcie discovered it. "But I walk down the beach every day."

"I remember how much you loved it."

"How's your mom, Marce?"

"She died a few years ago. Breast cancer. Pop didn't last long after that."

"God, honey, I'm so sorry."

"Well, we're all sorry about what happened with the parents. We missed you. And summer was never the same after we stopped coming up here."

"I know."

"Your mom got in contact after your dad died."

"Yeah. She told me."

"I've been thinking about getting in touch with you ever since. My sisters were merciless at Christmas."

"Is Aunt Jean…"

"Still alive and holding as big a grudge as ever."

Eva laughed. Her aunts had used the money when they'd sold Blue Heaven for college funds and big weddings for their kids. Neither of which had ever been even a possible in Eva's future. But now she had this.

Chapter Thirty-Two

Eva hardly believed what had happened. Daniel. He was always doing stuff for her. She was getting ready to head out to the store when he pulled up with two men. One guy had a camera and the other a digital voice recorder.

Daniel introduced them, but after meeting her cousins' spouses and children she spaced out immediately on the photographer's name. Eric? Lars? The writer, she knew, was William, because Daniel talked about him so much.

She shook their hands. "You're welcome to Kiwi and Blueberry cottages, to use for whatever you need. If you don't feel like driving back to Port Huron, feel free to stay. Otherwise, they're safe places to keep your equipment. We have a lot of kids on the premises this week."

William and his assistant took the keys she offered and went to inspect their work spaces.

"Daniel, will you hold down the fort while I zip to the grocery story?" Eva's words were light. Blue Heaven finally felt like home again, full of people she loved.

****

Her mom was awake when Eva returned from the store, sitting at the tiny kitchen table, looking out at the water. Bob had arrived, bringing Rock Band, which he was playing in the living room with Tyler and two local girls.

"What's the photographer's name?" Eva whispered to her mom over the din of The Beatles as she unpacked groceries.

"Boyd," her mom said, as William, Daniel, and Boyd came down from the airplane addition, Daniel telling the story of how Eva had insisted from the day he met her on that addition, but how he had "held out" until the blueprints had been located.

"We're going to take a drive through town," Daniel said, coming into the kitchen where Eva was loading a sack of potatoes and two large bowls onto the table.

"Barbecue at six," she reminded him.

"Yep," he said, kissing her and winking at her mom.

Eva searched through the drawer for a second potato peeler and handed it to her mother. They sat at the table, working at their task, listening to the music until the kids decided to go back outside.

Into the silence, her mother said "I like your young man very much."

"Me, too," Eva agreed.

"I hid those blueprints and letters in the shed," her mom admitted. "The day we came up to send your dad's ashes off."

Eva was puzzled.

"Why didn't you just give them to me?"

"I wasn't sure what was going to happen with the property. A few of your aunts had contacted a lawyer, saying that as Blue Heaven had always been in the Delacroix family, that upon your daddy's death, it should revert back to them."

"Mom! You never told me that."

"Well. It had nothing to do with your cousins. Just a couple of cantankerous old biddies. You remember how they picked this place clean when Daddy bought them out? Every piece of Depression glass, every Hall's bowl and milk glass pitcher? Well, Daddy secured the blueprints and letters back home, and nobody even inquired after that stuff. But I knew it was there, under our bed all these years. So when the lawyer contacted me, I found a tube and put the stuff in it and stuck it up in the shed. I figured whoever got the house should have the rest of it. Of course, I knew it would be you. But then I forgot about it. Glad you found it, dear."

"And the lawsuit?"

"Judge threw it out. Not a leg to stand on."

"My friend Jane brokered that deal." Ex-friend but Mom didn't need to hear that story. "She always dots the i's and crosses the t's." Eva got up and opened her cupboard, drawing out an ancient deep bowl, rimmed in orange flowers. The bowl had once had been white but had grayed with age.

"Our old potato salad bowl!"

"They go for upward of $50 in antique stores these days."

"My lord." He mother flipped the heavy bowl to inspect the gold Hall's stamp.

They steadily peeled the mountain of potatoes and had almost finished when the cousins came in, showered and ready to work. When Marcie entered the kitchen ten minutes later, it got a tad too crowded. Eva asked her mom if she'd like to sit on the new porch.

"Just let me beat this sour cream into the mayo."

"I'll mash the egg yolks," Marcie said, slicing into

a bowl of boiled eggs.

"Aunt Alice," Marcie said, adding the yolks to the mayo and sour cream mixture, "my mom made the same potato salad you did. I can cut up the green onions and celery for you."

"Thanks, dear." Eva's mom allowed her to lead her out to the porch.

They heard the voices rise from the beach and saw big water, blue to the horizon, where it almost matched the sky.

After a few minutes, Marcie came out with a stack of paper plates and asked where they were eating.

"Upstairs," Eva said.

"We aren't eating in the office like in the old days?"

"Have you seen it up there?" Georgie said, beer in hand. "It's perfect."

"We don't have the old table anymore anyway."

"My dad took it for a workbench," Georgie admitted.

Daniel was back from his tour, and had fired up the grill.

"Steaks in ten," he said.

"I'm not sure the potato salad will be cool enough by then," Eva's mom worried.

"It'll be great, Aunt Alice. I set it in the sink, full of ice. And then I put ice over the top of it too. After I wrapped it in foil, of course. Works every time."

Eva's mother did not look convinced, but nor did she look concerned. She took the stairs slowly, admiring the burnished wood of the banister Daniel had carved.

"Your young man is as talented as he is

handsome," her mom said.

Eva knew that, knew the list was even longer. Daniel was also kind, intelligent, creative, compassionate...and somewhat clueless about what it would take to make their relationship work. She kept thinking about the lack of condoms. Was he changing his mind about having a family?

"It's like a tree house up here," Paulette said. "All these windows."

"How your father would have loved this," Mom said, tears in her eyes.

Eva hugged her mom. She didn't want to let her go. Not today, not ever. But most of Mom's friends were in Sarasota now, and the winter weather there was kinder to her bones.

Everyone gathered like locusts at the full tables.

Eva opened a bottle of wine and offered it around. She poured a glass for herself and sat next to her mother. She still couldn't quite believe Mom was here.

"Just waiting on the steaks." Bob brought up a platter of burgers and hot dogs that the kids and a few of the men dug into. Eva and her mom sat on the sofa, a little apart from the rest of the family, but closer than they'd been in such a long time. It was more than enough for Eva, especially when Daniel, William, and Boyd appeared, Daniel laden with a huge platter of New York strips.

Dinner was just like Eva remembered it from all those years ago. The location had moved up, as had their ages, but the feeling of family love was the same.

****

After her cousins had departed from a week of sun and fun, Eva realized a trial run had been a good thing.

She'd figured out what worked (muffins and coffee in the morning) and what didn't (putting wet towels in the dryer before running them through the washing machine). Wanda, Luke's mother, had come by to help her clean on Friday, the morning of departure for everybody, including her mother, who missed the quiet of her condo in Florida and her mysterious friend Ernst.

"He's a dear man, and you'll meet him at Christmas," was all her mom would say about Ernst.

Because Wanda had things so clearly in hand with the laundry and the bathrooms and the rest of it, Eva was able to take her mom to the airport.

"He's a keeper," her mom said. Eva knew she was talking about Daniel. "It's about time I had some grandkids."

"I hope so, too, Mom."

"I predict he'll propose before Christmas. Then you can both come down to see me."

Eva just smiled. If only.

At the airport security checkpoint, with one final hug, Eva said, "I love you Mom."

"And honey, you know I love you. You're my girl."

Why did saying goodbye have to be so difficult? Would it be this bad when she had to say goodbye to Daniel in September? Would it be worse?

She drove back to Blue Lake and mentally prepared to spend a week living with her boyfriend. Playing house. She hadn't told her mother about that.

Chapter Thirty-Three

After giving her family the run of the bungalow, Eva felt more relaxed about letting guests use the house. She packed up her laptop and cell phone, some clothes and makeup, and then it hit her.

To do this properly, she'd have to clear out all of her personal things. Her guests would not like opening drawers to view Eva's nightgowns or blue jeans anymore than Eva wanted their eyes on her stuff.

She went out to the living room where Wanda vacuumed under sofa cushions.

"Do you know anybody in town who does house moving? Like with a small truck but boxes and those wardrobe things where you just transfer your clothes still on their hangers?"

"Walt Samson and his brother do that. 'Large Guys, Small Price.'" Wanda was already looking up the number in her cell phone directory.

"When do you need them?"

"Ten minutes ago."

Wanda spoke into the phone and then handed it to Eva, who explained her dilemma to Samson's wife, Rita.

Rita assured Eva that the men could fit in a quick run today. Just as she was disconnecting, she got a text message ping from Mr. Augustine. *Jane moved to a mental health facility while doctors determine if she is fit to stand trial.* Eva closed her phone and put it in her pocket.

By the time Large Guys got to Blue Heaven, Eva had piled all the clothes from her two dressers onto her bed. Her big suitcase was already full and stashed in her trunk. That had her week's wardrobe in it. This was everything else. The men made short work of boxing up her clothes, jewelry, and shoes while Eva cleared the bathroom cabinets and her private office papers.

She followed the truck to Daniel's and told the guys she'd be doing this all again in a week, in reverse. They didn't seem fazed. But she did. She had an uneasy feeling that this week would either make or break her relationship with Daniel.

"Hey, babe!" Daniel came out of the house. "Planning on making this a permanent move?" He was teasing her, but she thought it might not be the worst idea in the world.

"Sorry for all the stuff."

"No, that's fine. I get it."

"You guys can store everything upstairs." Daniel led the way to two bedrooms, one empty, one with a twin bed and dresser but nothing in the closets.

"I've got my personal stuff in my car," Eva said as they stepped out of the movers' way.

"You'll keep that in my room. I cleared one side of the closet for you. And some drawers."

"Thanks, sweetheart." She gave him a quick kiss that the movers caught on their way down for more of Eva's stuff.

"So you're okay with giving your quarters to strangers?"

"More than I thought I'd be." She wondered when

the right time to bring up their future would be. Probably not yet. Her makeup wasn't even on the dressing table yet. "Wanda said she'd look out for Mama and the kittens, but I miss them."

"Bring them here."

"Really?" *Good sign*, she thought. "I might have guests who are allergic. If I continue to rent out the bungalow."

The movers left and Daniel hauled her suitcase up the stairs while she took the lighter carry-on with her toiletries.

"What smells so good?"

"Salmon. Hungry?"

"I am. But I need to unpack first." He had his arm around her as they looked into the room. How she would love to give it a face-lift. Except for the bed, which was just fine.

"I'm the same. Got to get a feel for your new territory." He kissed her when he said it. "Please treat this as your home.

"There are three bathrooms up here," Daniel said. "Bob and I have bathrooms in our suites, and I thought you'd be more comfortable in the suite bathroom, so I had my cleaner move all my things to the bathroom across the hall." He pointed to a powder blue room on the other side of the hall from the bedroom they were standing in, the one that connected to Daniel's room. Since she'd last seen this room, he'd brought in an Art Deco dresser, a sweet velvet reading chair, a pretty reading lamp, and a vanity table. No bed. It was like a little sitting room.

"I thought this could be your dressing room."

"So where will I be sleeping?" She wanted to make

sure.

"With me." He sounded indignant and a little rattled. "Is that a problem?" He dropped her suitcase and put his arms around her waist. He touched his forehead to hers as if he was trying to read her mind.

"Well, there's Bob."

"He knows. He's fine."

She let him pull her all the way into his room and when he tugged her onto the bed with him, she went willingly. They rested that way, fully clothed, his arms around her, her head on his heart.

"I've never lived with anyone except my mom and dad," she said.

"Not even a roommate?"

"Nope."

"Well, except for my short time in college, I've only ever lived with Bob."

"It's just for a week," she said.

"Yep."

Then he kissed her and she ran her hands under his T-shirt, helping him take it off. She loved his body, so hard and muscled. They were naked when she remembered the food.

"It's on an automatic timer. It will turn off when it's done." And that was the last thing either of them said for a long time. When they finally got to it, the salmon was room temperature and they were starving.

She'd never had a meal at Daniel's. He had a huge island in the kitchen with stools, which is where they ate.

"Would Bryman approve of an island?"

Daniel shrugged. "It's functional. I update anything I think is really worth it. And feeding Bob all these years, this island is the only way I can get him to sit down. We never use the dining room. My parents used it every weekend, seems to me."

"But it's so pretty."

"Yes, well, feel free to organize a dinner party or anything else you'd like while you're here."

"Really?" Maybe that could be the special thing she'd do for Daniel. But it was hard to know. When would she be stepping over boundaries? "I'd like to know your friends better. Can we have a few couples, and maybe Luke and a few other singles?"

"Yes, of course. I want you to feel like this is your home, too."

This was more than she'd hoped for. He hadn't acted jealous over Luke. He trusted her. Of course, she wanted even more. But for Day One, she'd take it.

After they ate, they took a walk on the beach. Daniel's house was only a block from the water.

"I like having you in my house," he said.

"And I like being there." She pulled her cardigan tighter against the lake breeze as they walked. Not too far down that shoreline other people were sleeping in her house. It didn't feel quite like a home to her anymore. Would it ever again?

****

Eva got right to planning her dinner party, sitting in the dining room with a pad of paper and her cell phone. There was no way she'd survive an entire winter here without friends. Meg and Steve were free the next night. So was Luke, but his friend was not. Meg suggested a single female they all knew and liked.

"She's divorced," Meg said.

"Will Luke feel he's being set up?"

"I don't think so. Her divorce is recent and she's not any more interested in being set up than he is."

"Okay, so that's the six of us. Perfect number for my first dinner party."

"I'm so happy for you and Daniel. We were all shocked at how out of control Jane got when she went off her meds."

"The police report says she may not have gone off them, but was taking more than she should along with drinking way too much."

"Horrible for you."

"Yeah. We were tight. It hurt when she backstabbed me like that. But she's not well, and I need to let it go."

"Well, don't worry, I do not have the energy to plot any great drama like Jane, not that I'd ever want to."

Eva laughed and asked a few questions about menu things. Who was a vegetarian? Who didn't eat fish? Anybody hate broccoli? After talking to Meg, she felt a lightness that had been missing lately. Even with the family back together, she still hadn't been able to shake Jane's betrayal.

And she'd also realized that her family was not going to come back together in the way it had been before. She'd see them for one week in the summer, not for three months. And that was fine.

Her final entry in the "losing" column was Daniel. She'd be losing him to Georgia in a few short months. She had promised herself not to think about it, to live every day fully alive to the moment. Living that way really did help her to realize how happy she was. How fortunate. How deeply in love. And lots of lovers lived far apart these days. She didn't know how they did it, she didn't think she could stand it, but even more, she could not stand to lose Daniel.

****

The next day, Eva did all the shopping. A woman came to clean while she was on her way out. "She's been cleaning for us for twenty years." He gave Eva a brief kiss. "I'm going down to the museum, but my housekeeper knows her way around the place."

The three of them stood in the front parlor, a room rarely used but kept in grand readiness for special occasions, like a dinner party.

"I'll leave you to it, shall I?" Daniel quickly exited.

Eva explained to the housekeeper about her moving in, about the bungalow being rented to guests, and about how she would likely find messes and things out of place. "We're still organizing."

"Anything in particular you'd like me to do today?"

"Focus on the public spaces and leave the upstairs alone for now. If you could get out the good china and crystal and make sure none of it's dusty…"

"It's not!" The housekeeper seemed scandalized. "I keep the silver polished as well."

Eva smiled at her. "You're a wonder. I didn't even know there was sterling silver!"

The housekeeper opened a drawer in the dining room cabinet and flipped up a cloth to show gleaming forks and knives.

"And vases? I'll need a few for flowers."

"I'll have them ready for you." The housekeeper was already examining imaginary dust inside the china cabinet.

Eva drove forty miles out of her way to buy from a

store that had the freshest and the best meats, seafood, produce, and baked goods. Her car trunk already had a cooler full of ice for perishables. Daniel's idea.

When she got home, Daniel helped her unpack the car. "Thank you for making me feel so at home," she said. "I've been trying really hard to come up with something special for you. You've planned all our dates, and each one tops the next."

"Well, I'd never be able to organize a dinner party. But I damn well want Luke to see you are here, let him know you're with me. Not that he's out of his 'down with women' phase yet, but if anyone could bring him out of his funk, you could."

"What about someone named Holly Spring?"

"Ha! The pair of them will cry on each other's shoulders." Daniel's face went from farce to serious in seconds. "Don't know what I'd do if I ever lost you!"

"That's not going to happen." The truth was, neither of them knew what the future held.

They gave each other a big hug and a long kiss and then went each to their own tasks. Like newlyweds, just without the ring and the wedding and the legal documentation. Eva willed herself to think of what was happening now instead of what she wanted to happen in the future. Now was dinner party time.

The housekeeper bustled into the kitchen. "The house is done, but I'll stay and help you clean up pots and pans, if you like."

"That's so sweet of you! I decided to buy a ham. Then I'm making my Mom's potato salad, and I bought a yummy fruit tart thing for dessert. So, not much clean up. You go on home and put your feet up."

"Thank you, Eva. I was at your open house, you

know. What you have done for this town, well, we all love you like you're one of our own, honey."

"Aw. Thanks." Eva was not sure about the etiquette of hugging the hired help, so she put her hands together in prayer pose and did a little bow. In yoga, they followed that with "namaste" which means, very loosely translated, have a good day.

"Well, dear, everything you need is in here. Just look around and get your bearings. And call me if you can't find something. Leave the mess for me to come in and clean in the morning."

"Oh, but why? That doesn't seem fair."

"Daniel pays me overtime for cleaning up after parties." This was said in a tone that indicated she preferred the overtime cash.

"Well then, of course I'll leave the clean up to you."

"You are so good for Daniel. He has never had a lady friend over for dinner. And certainly not anyone to live in! Only had football things, with the guys. Lots of dips and chips and beer mugs. I like to see him moving on. You're the reason he's starting to settle down."

"Well, I'm only moving in for a week. Because I've rented out the bungalow."

"Loads of people have been asking me about that. They want reservations! You should think about it. There's plenty of room here and once you and Daniel set up house it would be a shame to just have it end in a week."

Eva was touched. Her eyes welled a bit. "Thank you," she said. "I love him very much."

"I know he loves you too, my dear. This is the start of something very special. I always know these things.

And that's why you must stay. Talk to Daniel."

Of course they'd talk, but Eva didn't want to mention the part about renting out the bungalow and living together all summer. They needed to discuss that maybe, if things went well this week.

But no more thinking about the future. She was having her first ever dinner party. She needed to get to work. The ham was simple. It was a spiral cut thing with a brown sugar glaze. She really didn't even have to bake it. She could make her mom's potato salad blindfolded. And all she had to do with the fruit and cheese platter was make sure the cheese was out about an hour before company arrived. Easy as pie. Not that she'd ever actually made a pie.

She cooled the white wine and chose a few reds from Daniel's stash of thirty or so bottles. He'd given her full access, and since she knew nothing about wine, she picked the ones with the most writing on the label. And made sure they were French.

Maybe one or two bottles were special. And he'd forgotten to tell her. She called him , hoping he wouldn't think she was a pain.

"Hi honey, what's up?"

Honey. Well, she guessed he didn't feel as if she were bothering him after all.

"I just have these French red wines, and I know I need to open them to breathe, but I wondered if you had any special bottles you didn't want opened?"

"Nope. Don't you know you're worth the best wine in the world? Not that I have any of that on hand." He laughed. She relaxed.

"Okay then, thanks."

"Love you."

He said "love you" in front of the work crew. She could clearly hear them, so they must be able to hear him. "Love you, too." That felt good to say.

After they hung up, she remembered she'd bought an apron and had totally forgotten to put it on. She checked her list. Everything was set except the roasted vegetables. Eva had never roasted vegetables. She'd bought beets and carrots and onions, because she'd asked Daniel his favorites and those were what he liked. She had a recipe that didn't seem particularly difficult. She decided to get ready first, just in case someone came early, then set the table, then get the vegetables in the roaster. Oh shoot! The bread. She'd bought brown-and-serve rolls and the temperature for them was different than the one on the recipe for the veggies. She'd figure something out. Unlike Jane, Daniel didn't have two ovens.

****

Relaxed from her bath, she dressed with care and used a light touch of makeup. Her hair had been super frizzy as she ran around the kitchen, so she wrapped it up in a messy twist.

Setting the table with fine linens and exquisite china made her remember she hadn't ordered flowers. Did she have time? God! Everyone would be here in less than an hour. And where was Daniel? She told herself to take a chill pill, but that didn't really work unless you actually took a pill.

She called Daniel again.

"Everything okay?" From the sound of his voice, she knew he was on the blue-tooth phone in his car. On his way home.

"Yes, but, I'm so sorry to be such a bother." She'd

wanted to pull off this dinner party like it was second nature. She wanted everything perfect. She felt an utter fool to have forgotten flowers.

"You're not a bother. I like you needing me. What can I do?"

"Pick up flowers?"

"Not a problem."

"Are you sure?"

"I'm sure. And anything else you need before I get home, you just call and ask. I am yours to command."

She giggled. "Even later, after everyone's gone?"

"Even then," he said in a low sexy tone.

They hung up eventually and she didn't feel quite so bad anymore about bugging him. He absolutely wanted to be consulted on every little detail she felt unsure of. He was a keeper.

After thirty minutes with no Daniel, she got worried. Does choosing flowers take that much time? And Daniel time *was* a little different from clock time, especially when he was involved in one of his beloved restorations. She hoped he hadn't gone back to the site. And really, had she been sure he was in his car when she'd talked to him?

She sat down and took a few deep breaths. She was being silly over nothing. She did not need to call him again. He would be here. On time. With flowers.

She got up and pulled herself together. Okay, where had she put that apron? She found it still in the store bag tucked in the laundry room. She pulled it out, cut the price tag off and wrapped it around her waist. She got the oven pre-heating. Roasting called for a high temperature. 425 degrees. That couldn't be right. She checked Google on her phone.

According to FoolProofCook.com, the temperature was right for roasting. Okay, then. She scrubbed the veggies, then peeled and cubed them. The carrots and onions were easy, but the beets were so hard to do she ended up not peeling them except to trim off the ends. Then she quartered them.

As she oiled the beet quarters, one of them flew to the right and hit the refrigerator on it's way to the floor, the other did a ricochet into the dining room, leaving a big red stain on an antique tablecloth and a broken crystal wine glass that probably cost $200. There were more wine glasses, so she cleaned the glass up and got another one out of the cabinet, but she still felt bad.

At least the flowers would cover the stain. Or should she re-do the table and get to work on the stain? Probably or it would never come out.

She could feel herself winding up with anxiety again as she stacked the dishes and took the tablecloth into the laundry room along with the housekeeper's phone number. She answered and told Eva exactly what to use, a mixture she kept on the shelf in the laundry room.

"You want to soak it overnight and I'll take care of the rest of it in the morning."

"Will it be okay?"

She promised it would be fine, and added that there were lots of tablecloths, all old and cherished, and Eva could find another one in the linen closet just off the pantry with the napkins and rings.

Napkins and rings? She'd set out paper napkins. Okay, she saw the napkins and threaded them through the shiny silver rings.

Daniel came in just then without flowers.

Right behind him were Meg and Steve. Followed shortly by Luke and Holly. Crap. She'd forgot to set out the cheese. Still, she had to greet them. She was the hostess.

"Hi!" She put enthusiasm into her hug for Daniel, but he held her a bit away from himself.

"Is that beet juice on your apron?"

She blushed. She had forgotten to take the damn apron off. Well, she still needed it on, because she had to mix the vegetables with some olive oil. She hadn't quite got the rolls sorted yet either. Still, she had to carry on, carry this off.

"Hi everyone! Sorry things are a little chaotic."

"Just going to dash up for a shower," Daniel said. Nobody acted like that was in any way odd.

"Come on in." Eva asked for drink orders as she held her hands to indicate that they should all sit in the front parlor. Nobody got the gesture and they all followed her through the dining room into the kitchen and gathered around the island.

"Eva, do you want me to set the table?" Meg asked.

"No way. You put your feet up and relax."

Everyone stood at the butcher block while Eva poured wine and handed out beers and got Meg a fruit juice she'd bought special. They showed no signs of leaving the kitchen, so she put all her chopped veggies in a bowl and removed them from the island. She popped the cheese tray down with some pretty grapes on the side. She threw a basket of crackers together, and got them in, too, darting between elbows. Finally, she handed Holly a dish of salted nuts. "Can you squeeze these in there?"

Then she went to the area by the sink and oven and finished prepping those damned beets.

"Wow, looks like a few of your beets took a flier," Luke said. She noticed the areas splashed red and threw him a damp cloth.

"Could you get those before they set?"

Everyone laughed at that. "You'll fit right in here, Eva." Meg beamed at her. "We like to keep the men on their toes."

"Well, my man forgot the flowers!" Eva said, while finally spreading the ridiculously work-intensive vegetables on a baking sheet and sliding them into the oven.

"Oh, sorry, sweetie." Daniel came down from the shower, his hair still wet. The doorbell rang. "I'll get it."

Eva wondered if he'd invited more guests, but he walked through the dining room with a huge bouquet. "Where do you want these?"

She should never have doubted him.

"Do you know where the vases are?"

Daniel looked stumped. Holly got up and searched the upper shelves of the pantry. "In here. Luke come help. I'm too short to reach." There was a smashing sound of breaking glass. "Sorry!" Holly called out as she returned to the kitchen with a beautiful vase of blue glass.

By then Daniel had opened the flower arrangement and they discovered it already had a vase.

"I'll just need a broom," Luke said, coming in with a sheepish look on his face. "Hope it wasn't an heirloom."

"Everything in this place is an heirloom." The

words were out of Eva's mouth before she knew she'd said them.

Eight eyes looked at her, not sure how to take her words. "I love old things, but I get nervous when they're valuable."

"Not to worry, my love," Daniel said, coming to her side and kissing her on the temple. "Can I get another round here? And one for the hostess."

Eva gratefully accepted the glass of wine and the help as everyone pitched in. She conferred with Holly on the vegetable/roll issue and Holly suggested that she bake the rolls while the vegetables kept warm in a separate part of the oven Eva hadn't even known was there.

Eva drank a little wine and ate a little cheese and crackers and then went back in to tackle the tablecloth dilemma. She found another one and got the entire table up and looking swank again in a jiffy.

"Daniel, do you have candles?"

He produced a pair of crystal holders, complete with candles already inserted, from a cupboard over the fridge that was way too high for her to reach. She took the candles and asked him to bring in the flowers. The table looked splendid.

Daniel put his arm around her. "You did good, kid."

"Thanks. I got a spiral cut ham. You think you can cut some onto a platter for us?"

"No problem. Let's just relax a bit first with the gang."

"Well, yes, there's an hour until the roast vegetable are done, so no hurry."

Her voice must have sounded fretful, because he

said, "And that's why they call it cocktail hour." Then he kissed her again, this time on the lips. Then they went to join their friends.

Daniel got everyone refills and proposed a toast. "You are here because Eva is here, and we are honored to have you to our very first dinner party."

The cocktail hour continued until the timer rang for the vegetables. Eva was more at ease after her glass of wine. She found a bowl and serving spoon while Daniel cut the ham. Holly popped the rolls into the oven and Meg lay down in the parlor because her back hurt. "She'll lie like that five minutes," Steve said, "and then she'll be right as rain. You'll see."

The rolls were a little too brown on the bottom, and the ham actually could have done with a bit of warming, but everyone loved the potato salad. Just as Steve had predicted, Meg was fine at dinner. Eva beamed at the people around the table. These were her future friends. She knew it, and it made her feel warm inside, despite the overcooked dinner rolls and the under-warmed ham.

Everyone tried to see each other on the other side of the table over the massive arrangement of flowers until Daniel got up and put them in the parlor. Eva brought out the fruit tart and Daniel made coffee when Meg let out a squeak.

"Oh no! I'm afraid we'll never be invited again. Luke broke a vase. Holly ruined the rolls, and now I've gone and broken my water all over your pretty antique chair." Meg put her hands into her face and sobbed.

"Your water?" Steve jumped up and was at Meg's side.

"Honey, that's nature," Daniel said. "No worries

about the chair, please."

"Oh! The baby's coming. I feel honored to be present at the moment birth begins." Eva was thinking about her own babies. She and Daniel had stopped using condoms. He had not asked if she was on the pill. She wasn't. She should tell him.

"Do you have any huge panties and jeans I might borrow. I think we need to go to the hospital. I was looking forward to that tart, too!"

Eva and Meg went upstairs while the rest of the company closed their eyes on Meg's pleading insistence. "I'm so happy for you!" Eva said, pulling out a pair of Daniel's boxers and fairly new sweat pants.

"Your turn next." Meg grinned.

After seeing the giddy couple off, they were a cozy foursome. They ate the tart and drank the coffee, and Eva had high hopes for Luke and Holly, but they left, each in their own bubble of loneliness, soon after dessert.

Eva and Daniel waved at them out the front door. She couldn't get over how natural and right it felt to be in Daniel's house, by his side.

"It didn't go too bad, did it?" Eva hoped Daniel felt as cozily domestic as she did.

"It was excellent. I had fun. I think we all did."

"Well, I broke a wine glass that looks like it cost hundreds of dollars and spilled beet juice on the best tablecloth, but other than that, it was all good."

"Excellent." Daniel swooped her up and into his arms and started for the stairs.

Cynthia Harrison

Chapter Thirty-Four

They picked up Mama and the kittens the next day. Only Salt and Pepa were left, as she'd let her cousins' kids each have one of the others.

A few days later, while the kittens played with red ribbon, Daniel asked about Christmas.

"I promised my mom I'd come see her at Christmas. I need to meet her boyfriend." Eva laughed, but her heart was not light at the thought. "I wish we could be together."

"I can fly Bob down to Sarasota. We'll rent a condo. Then we'll all be together. I like living with you."

"I like it, too."

****

"What would you think if I stayed here for now?" Eva asked, a few days later, over breakfast. Daniel must have swallowed a crumb of his toast down the wrong pipe, because instead of answering, he did a kind of choking cough. He drank orange juice and then loudly cleared his throat.

"Why?"

Not quite the response she'd hoped for.

"Wanda's been fielding requests. I'd like to continue to rent the bungalow out on a weekly basis." That wasn't the whole story but she had to come at this thing slowly. She had to know if he wanted things to go in the same direction she wanted. "Plus if I wasn't running Blue Heaven, I could start on the museum."

"But Blue Heaven was your dream…"

"It was my dad's dream. It was a way for me to support myself. I realized after living here in town with you for a few days that I like it better than living next to a state park and taking care of vacationers. I can get Wanda some help, and Blue Heaven will still support me, but I don't have to live there."

He nodded and pushed his plate of food, only half-finished, away. "I like the idea of starting the museum project now."

She ran both their plates under water at the sink. "Ow." The water had gotten too hot. She dropped the breakfast plate. At least it didn't break. He probably didn't want her to move in because lots of things seemed to get broken when she was around.

"So how would that work? You'd stay here in this house while I'm in Georgia? Or would you buy your own house here in town?"

She turned from the sink back to him, drying her hands on a dishtowel, her heart repeatedly trying to leap into her throat.

"I don't like the idea of you being here alone all winter." He stopped for a minute and she could see his mind tumbling with possible responses. "But I like it better than you staying at Blue Heaven with six vacant cottages."

"I know. Even having Luke there to keep the snow off the roof tops and Wanda doing a daily check, it still seems like it would be too isolated." She thought for a minute. "Maybe I could get a house of my own closer to Luke's or Meg's place. That way I wouldn't be so lonely."

She didn't mean for Daniel to get upset when she mentioned Luke, but he walked out of the kitchen without another word. Damn. He came back a few minutes later, car keys in hand.

"I'm going into PH for some things." He didn't ask her if she wanted to come with him like he normally would.

"Okay."

Eva didn't cry easily, but when she heard Daniel's car fire up, she burst into angry sobs. Or maybe, as her tears began to wind down, they were sad sobs. She sat on the sofa and let it all out. Of course Mama, Salt, and Pepa all came to comfort her.

She cried herself out and must have fallen asleep, because Daniel was there, in the living room, asking her a question. Or saying something.

"Sorry." She sat up, careful to move Mama from her reclining lap. "What?"

"Have you been crying? Your eyes are all red."

"Oh, well." She was silent. Humiliated.

Daniel paced up and down the room, his body full of tension. She'd blown it. He kept raking his hands through his hair and shaking his head. She'd taken a chance on his feelings, and it had been a disaster.

Daniel continued to pace the room. At least he wasn't asking what she'd cried about. "I'm sorry, but I really don't want you to stay here this winter." Daniel finally stopped pacing and sat next to her on the sofa. He took her into his arms, holding her close. "Don't you know how much I love you?"

She didn't. "I know you love me, and I love you, but I'm not sure how much."

"More than anything."

Her eyes, probably puffy as well as red from the marathon cry earlier, opened wide. She looked at his hand holding hers. Slowly, she moved her gaze upward until their eyes met. Then she threw herself at him in a hug that almost knocked him off the sofa. "I love you more than anything too."

"We get along." He was holding her as tightly as she held him.

"We do." Now she pulled a little bit away and put her head on his shoulder.

"So would you come with me to Georgia? Then we wouldn't have to be apart."

She hadn't let herself think this far ahead. Well, not much anyway. "Yes, I'll come to Georgia with you."

"And will you marry me, too?" He let one knee drop to the floor, took a small velvet box from his pocket, opened it. A pink diamond. Several carats, but not too many. It looked vintage. It sparkled in the sun as he removed it from the box. "This was my mother's ring. I had it sized and cleaned. That's where I went just now."

She held out her hand for Daniel to slip it on her finger. "You have to say yes first."

"I want to, but I need you to agree that we can have children. After we're married."

"Okay," he said.

"Then, yes."

He slipped the ring on her finger. Perfect fit. They kissed and then he snapped a photo of her ring finger and sent it to all their friends with a message *She said Yes!*

A word about the author...

In her twenty-year career as an English teacher, Cynthia Harrison published an award-winning writing manual she uses in her popular creative writing classes. She has published hundreds of reviews, features, and short fiction in *Romantic Times*, *Publishers Weekly,* and *Woman's World.*

Her first novel with The Wild Rose Press, *The Paris Notebook*, garnered praise on Amazon and review sites. Cindy has made a free story of two minor characters in *The Paris Notebook* available free on her website at:

www.cynthiaharrison.com.